D0545328

Also by Penny Joelson

I Have No Secrets
Nominated for the CILIP Carnegie Children's Book Award
Winner of the FCBG Children's Book Award for older readers
Winner of the Leeds Book Award
Winner of the Sussex ABA Award
Winner of the Worcestershire Teen Book Award
Winner of the Cumbria Book Award
Winner of the Bolton Book Award
Winner of the Bristol Book Award
Winner of the St Helens Book Award
Winner of the Girls' Day School Trust Book Award
Winner of the Trinity Schools Book Award

Girl in the Window
Winner of the North East Book Award

THINGS THE EYE CAN'T SEE

PENNY JOELSON

First published in Great Britain in 2020
by Electric Monkey, an imprint of Egmont UK Limited
2 Minster Court, London EC3R 7BB

Text copyright © 2020 Penny Joelson

The moral rights of the author have been asserted

ISBN 978 1 4052 9491 1

A CIP catalogue record for this title is available from the British Library

70444/001

Printed and bound in Great Britain by CPI Group

Typeset by Avon DataSet Ltd, Arden Court, Alcester, Warwickshire

To my nephews and niece,
Asher, Sammy and Layla

1

The voice startles me because it sounds like Charlie. I'm good at recognising voices, but it can't be him, can it? Charlie used to be in my form group at school, but no one's seen him for about six months. I'm down a quiet path – not far from my house. He's calling my name.

I move my camera from my eye and stand upright. The poppy on the grassy verge, the one I was about to photograph with my macro lens, shape-shifts from perfect crimson petals around deep dark stamens to a slight fleck of red. I can only see clearly one or two centimetres in front of my eyes. My guide dog Samson shuffles beside me and stands as if expecting us to move on.

'Wait, Samson,' I say, pulling gently on his harness as I turn in the direction of the voice. Someone's there, but he's just a vague, dark blob.

'Libby!'

He says it again – my name. His voice distinctive, gravelly, but sounding older than I remember. He's coming nearer and the blur of him is familiar: the height, taller than me, light hair, the way he moves. It's him – now I'm as sure as I can be. But I'm not sure if I want to talk to him – or if I ought to.

'Charlie? Is it really you?'

I feel a pull as Samson turns too, his warm back nudging at my legs. 'Sit, Samson,' I tell him. 'Sit.' Samson sits obediently and I stroke his head.

'Yeah . . .' Charlie's close now. He sounds nervous, awkward – and I'm not surprised.

'Where've you been all this time?' I demand. 'You just dropped out of school. No one knew why.'

When he speaks his voice is low, bitter, emphatic. 'Stuff . . . life . . . y'know?' he says. 'Things happen.'

'I guess,' I say.

'And you,' he says. 'You got a dog now!'

'Yeah – this is Samson,' I tell him.

'He's lovely. You're lovely, boy!' he says to Samson. 'I like dogs.' He sounds sad now, wistful.

'What happened, Charlie? Can't you tell me?'

'Na. But . . . I want to ask you something – a favour.'

2

My heart speeds up, wondering what he could possibly want. Perhaps I should have ignored him. I've always felt nervous around Charlie. He got excluded from school for fighting – more than once. He was sent to a referral unit for a while, for kids who can't cope in school. Then he came back – only for about a month – and then he disappeared. No one knew where he'd gone. The truth is, no one cared all that much. School was calmer; there was far less tension without him.

'What?' I ask nervously.

'D'you think you can take a message for me – give it to someone?'

'Can't you just DM them? Or text or something?' I ask.

'Nah. This is too sensitive. Top secret – and I can't trust most people, but I trust you. I can, can't I? Right?'

'I guess . . . What's this all about, Charlie?'

'And you mustn't tell anyone you've seen me,' he goes on. 'You get that?'

'Are you serious? Why?' I wish I could see his face, but I'd need to get too close to really see his eyes.

'You gotta swear – this is dead serious,' he says.

3

I can hear the desperation in the raspy tone of his voice. My mind slips back to one time at school when he was kind and helped me out. It was last year, before I got Samson. I was walking down the stairs with my cane and some impatient boy kicked it out of the way. I nearly fell – but Charlie was there and he caught me and gave the boy a right earful. I was a bit shaky and he was really sweet. I'd never seen that side of him before.

'Please,' he begs.

'OK. I swear I won't tell anyone.' I say it – though I'm not sure I should, or if I mean it. 'What's the message?'

'Here.' He touches my arm, presses something into my hand. A small envelope. I hold it – at arm's length initially, as if it might explode.

'Put it away – in your pocket,' he tells me.

I feel for my skirt pocket and slip the envelope in.

'That's right,' he tells me. 'Now give it to Kyle at school tomorrow, OK?'

'Kyle?' I repeat.

'Yeah, don't tell him you saw me or that I gave it you. Just give it to him quiet, like. You got it?'

Kyle's the tallest boy in our year. Even I

4

can generally pick him out.

'OK,' I tell him.

'I knew I could trust you,' he says. 'I knew you'd help.'

'Charlie . . .' I start, but the blur of him is moving away and in an instant he's gone from my vision.

I finger the straight edges of the envelope in my pocket. I'm anxious. I wish I'd said no – but part of me also feels chuffed that he's chosen me for this task. He's not seeing me as 'the blind girl' like most people do – but as someone who can help him, someone he can trust. It's nice, in a weird sort of way.

I want to go home. 'Forward,' I tell Samson and he walks on eagerly, but my legs don't seem to want to move and I stop. Samson stops too and nudges me in confusion as if to say, 'Come on!'

I can hardly believe what just happened. My friend Madz is going to lose it when I tell her. But I shouldn't tell her, should I? I promised Charlie. I wish I hadn't promised that.

The flowers in the long grass are swaying, the dots of colour catching my eye as if beckoning me. I'm still holding my camera, so I lean over and take a few more close-ups, breathing deeply, calming myself until I feel ready to move.

'OK, Samson,' I tell him. 'Forward. Yes – we're going home.'

Samson's up instantly and guiding me towards home. It's a bright, warm day in early June, but something makes me shiver. I'm still thinking about Charlie. Why did he turn up here today? And what is in the note for Kyle?

2

When we get home, I ring the doorbell because I know Gran will be there and it's easier than fiddling around with my key. My brother Joe should be home too.

'Hi Libby!' says Gran, opening the door. 'You're late. I was getting worried.'

'Only a couple of minutes!' I come in and take off Samson's harness. 'Good dog. Well done,' I tell him, rubbing his head. Samson wags his tail against me and then pads off to the kitchen for a drink.

'How was your day?' says Gran, her voice softening. 'D'you want a cup of tea?'

'Ok, Gran – just a quick one,' I tell her. 'I've got tons of homework.'

I don't mind a short natter with Gran, but sometimes it's hard to get away. I've tried to tell Mum and Dad that I don't need her here every day after school – and neither does Joe. I'm fifteen and he's thirteen. We're fine on our own. Mum works long hours, but Dad teaches at a primary school so he's not back that late.

Mum gets it. She's always wanted me to be as independent as possible. She said it was fine for Gran to stop coming – but then Dad got involved and he said he feels happier knowing Gran's here. I was cross because I don't want to be treated differently just because I'm visually impaired – but Dad explained that Gran is lonely and likes to feel useful. He said she'd be gutted if he told her we didn't need her any more.

I can hear water gushing from the tap as Gran fills the kettle in the kitchen. I take the note from my skirt pocket and zip it into the front pocket of my school rucksack, before putting that on the bench by the front door where it lives. Everything has its place. I can't be tripping over things all the time, or hunting them down because I can't remember where I put them.

'Here you go, love,' says Gran, as I come into the kitchen. I reach for my usual chair and sit down at the kitchen table. I can hear Samson lapping water noisily from his bowl in the corner. Gran pushes a mug towards me and guides my hand to it.

'Be careful, that's hot,' she says, as if I might not know. 'Want a biscuit too? They're shortbread.'

She holds out a plate and I take one. The best thing about Gran being here is her homemade shortbread.

'Is Joe home?' I ask, taking a bite and letting it melt gently in my mouth.

'Yes – upstairs, like always,' Gran sighs. 'Hardly get a word out of him these days. But as long as he doesn't bring any of those creatures down here . . .'

Joe, who goes to a different school and gets home before me, somehow manages to whisk himself off to his room without getting caught up with Gran. I don't think Gran minds because it's not easy having a conversation with Joe. He's not exactly sociable. He used to be obsessed with computer games, but Mum and Dad got worried about it and decided to get him a pet as a distraction. Joe chose an iguana. Now Joe is reptile mad and has a room full of tanks and assorted creatures. He still hardly ever comes out.

'Tell me all about your day,' says Gran.

This is the bit I hate. Not much interesting happens, and even if it did, I'd not want to be telling Gran every detail. She always manages to say something that annoys me. Anyway, if I told her about Charlie and the note, she'd demand that I show her and she'd have no qualms about opening and reading it. She'd take over completely. It crosses my mind that maybe I should open it and read it myself with my magnifier. I'm tempted. I'd love to know what it says – but I promised. I can hear Charlie saying how he trusts me; I remember the desperation in his voice. Somehow, I don't want to let him down.

'English was good,' I tell Gran. 'We're reading *Pride and Prejudice*. And I've got art tomorrow. I'm looking forward to getting on with my painting.'

Gran tuts. 'Why you want to do art when you can barely see, I'll never understand,' she says. 'Wouldn't you rather do music? There are some amazing blind pianists, you know.'

This is Gran at her most irritating.

'Gran!' I protest. 'I love art – and photography – and I've never wanted to play the piano! Mum says . . .'

'Oh, please don't start telling me what your mother says,' Gran interrupts, sighing. 'She and I will never agree. I hear she's off to one of her conferences again next week? Where is it? Amsterdam, did your dad say?'

'Yes.'

'How long is it for this time?' Gran's disapproving tone is so obvious it makes me cross.

'Five days, I think,' I tell her. 'But we'll be fine. It's important work that she's doing. I'm proud of her, Gran. She's trying to make a difference – to help to save this planet!'

Mum's an engineer, developing environmentally friendly alternatives to plastic, and she gets asked to speak all over the world.

'Yes, but you and Joe are important too,' Gran insists. 'She should get her priorities straight. He needs help, that brother of yours – spending all his time stuck in that room with those reptiles. It can't be healthy. And you're doing well, Libby, but you're only just getting used to having a guide dog. Your mum should be helping you.'

I love Gran, but I've had enough of biting my tongue for one day. I stand up and push my chair back. 'I'd better get on with my homework.'

'Yes, I guess you had,' says Gran, sighing. 'But before you go – guess who I bumped into today?'

11

'Who?'

'Dominic!' Gran exclaims. 'Would you believe it – after all this time!'

Gran goes to a Book Group at U3A (University of the Third Age – classes for old people) on Thursdays and had started getting friendly with a guy called Dominic. We teased her because she seemed to bring his name into every conversation for a while, though she insisted they were 'just good friends'. But then he stopped coming, and they turned out not to be such 'good friends' because they hadn't even exchanged contact details so she had no way of keeping in touch. I wondered secretly whether he'd stopped because he got fed up with Gran, though I know that was a mean thought. He wasn't young, and it also seemed possible that he might have died.

'So where's he been?' I asked.

'In hospital, poor soul. He had a heart attack, but he's doing fine now. He'll be back at the group next week, he says. And he asked if I'd like to meet him for coffee tomorrow!'

'Ooh, Gran! Did you say yes?'

''Course I did!' Gran chuckles. Then she adds, 'I'd like to see you finding yourself a nice fella –

someone who'll look after you.'

'Gran!' I exclaim. 'I don't want or need some boy to *look after me*! And I don't want a boyfriend right now, anyway.'

'Sorry, sweetheart – have I put my foot in it again?' Gran says. 'Of course, there's no rush, you're right. I was sixteen when I met your granddad though,' she adds. 'And it might be harder for you – to find someone who'll be prepared to . . .'

'Gran!' I exclaim again before she can finish that sentence.

I can hear Dad's voice in my head saying, '*I know she doesn't always say the right things, but she means well, Libs. Her heart's in the right place.*' But Gran really does go too far sometimes – and this is one of those times. I open my mouth to tell her how I feel, but then I close it again. Gran hurt my feelings, but hurting hers back won't make it better.

'I'm off upstairs,' I tell her, and I go. Samson pads up the stairs behind me. I think he's had enough of Gran too.

I sit at my desk and open my BrailleNote – it's a laptop which converts my work from Braille to print and vice versa. So I can type Braille and print out a text version for the teacher to mark. I can also convert online handouts into Braille. I used to prefer to enlarge everything or use a magnifier, but now I have to do so much reading and writing, I've got faster at Braille and it's much quicker and less strain on my eyes.

Samson curls up by my feet while I try to get on with my history homework – but my mind keeps slipping back to Charlie and the note. I wonder what it says, and I'm tempted once again to open it. But I'd have to go back downstairs to get it – and anyway, I promised. I wonder how I'm going to give it to Kyle without anyone else knowing. I wonder what kind of trouble Charlie's in. I feel a nervous kind of excitement in the pit of my tummy. This isn't the sort of thing that happens in my very ordinary life. Everything's routine – at home and at school, going from lesson to lesson. But now I have a challenge – a task that takes me out of my normal zone.

Maybe I shouldn't have stopped when Charlie called my name. Maybe I shouldn't have taken the note. I could have said 'no'. But I didn't.

3

I'm walking to school, telling Samson, 'Straight on,' so he guides me along the road. Today I don't feel like going down the path that cuts through to the station, where I was when Charlie gave me the note yesterday. The sun's bright and I enjoy the warmth on my face. Cars zoom past one after the other, a constant hum. This, along with the smooth, hard pavement underfoot, feels reassuring right now, even though I usually prefer the birdsong of my usual route, with the occasional rattle of a train passing nearby, and the gravel, grass-edged path. There's nothing to stop and photograph here.

I've put the note back in my skirt pocket, but it feels like it's burning a hole. I'm still wondering what's going on with Charlie, and also why and how Kyle is involved. He's not exactly a friend of Charlie's. I've never been aware of them hanging out. Kyle's a bit off my radar. He doesn't say much, so I don't really notice him. The only thing I've noticed is his height. I've been paired with him a couple of times for projects and he has a nice voice, but he's a bit of a loner and he seems to be absent from school more than most. He's never been in trouble though – not even a detention for late homework as far I know.

My challenge is to somehow approach Kyle and give him the note without attracting attention. It isn't going to be easy. I might think that he's on his own, but there could be a bunch of people nearby who I don't even know are there and who can see everything.

I always meet my best friend Madz at the school gate. I want to tell her. I wasn't going to, but as I get closer to school I think maybe I will. I can trust Madz – and it would be a lot easier to do this with her help.

'Hey Libs! Hey Samson!' Madz is in her usual spot on the wall. She jumps down to greet me.

'Hi Madz. You all right?'

'Yeah. But last night was a disaster!'

'Why?' I ask.

'I think I've made a mess of things with Ollie.'

'Oh – what happened?' I ask.

'You know I was meeting him to see that film?'

I do know this. I was actually a bit peeved because I wanted to go to the film with Madz. And yes – I do enjoy the cinema. Once, when I had just started secondary school, a group of girls that I was hanging out with arranged to go to the cinema and didn't even tell me, as they thought I'd be upset to be left out. When I told them I could have used headphones and audio-description (a voice describes the action through the headphones) and that I love going to the cinema, they were completely shocked. At least they didn't leave me out again after that.

Madz and I go to the cinema quite often – or we did, until Ollie came on the scene three weeks ago. Now he's all that Madz can talk about. I don't want to be jealous of her having a boyfriend, but sometimes it's difficult.

'So what happened?' I ask.

'I only went to the wrong cinema, Libs! I went to the Vue and Ollie had booked for the Odeon!'

'Oh no! What did you do?'

'I felt such an idiot. I waited for ages – and then I called him, and I couldn't believe it! I said I'd get the next bus, but he said it was crazy to miss the beginning

17

and he'd get his mate to come instead. I'm gutted, Libby. I've got to find him now and make sure things are OK between us. I'm scared he thinks I'm stupid or that I wasn't bothered enough to turn up. You don't mind, do you?'

'No, sure,' I say. 'He'll be OK about it, won't he?'

'I hope so – I'll see you at registration.'

'Yes,' I say, as we reach the doors.

'Great.' She touches my shoulder gently. And then she's gone.

Someone shoves past me and I call out, 'Hey, watch it!'

I hate the crowded corridors first thing in the morning. I direct Samson towards our form room and he leads me there, carefully weaving in and out of the crowds. I'm relieved when we reach the room and I'm in my chair, with Samson snuggled under the desk by my legs. I didn't get to tell Madz about Charlie, and now I'm thinking about it, I'm glad I didn't. I don't need her help with this. I want to do it myself.

Five minutes later, Madz sneaks in beside me just as Miss Terri starts the register.

'Well?' I whisper.

'He's cool. I'm so relieved!' she whispers back. 'He's asked me to watch him play cricket at lunch. Would you mind? Can you manage without me?'

'You're not my carer,' I remind her. 'I'll be fine.'

I'm irritated that she thinks I can't cope without her, but also that she didn't ask me to join her. Not that I want to sit around at a cricket match.

Samson shuffles against my feet, as the implications of what she said start to filter through. I start to worry. Lunch in the dining hall is much easier with Madz. I don't have to think too much because she always finds us a table, and makes sure I don't put my lunch down too close to the edge, and that there's an empty chair so I'm not sitting on someone's bag where they've saved a seat.

I have other friends, but not close like Madz, and everyone has their lunch groups and routines. I'd feel awkward saying, 'Can I sit with you at lunch?' to Kaeya or Lilly. And then I'd have to ask them for that little bit of help too, but without them fussing over me. Madz does everything with no fuss. I forget she's even doing it.

'Are you OK? I feel really bad,' Madz says.

'It's fine,' I assure her. 'You've got to have a life.

19

I'm happy for you. I have to get used to doing stuff without you.'

I'm used to spending a lot of time with Madz – before school, lunchtimes, at least one night after school each week and one day at the weekend. I've never wanted her to feel that I'm relying on her. Our friendship hasn't felt like that. Being with her is effortless and I don't have to explain anything. Yet now she's got a boyfriend and isn't going to be around so much, I feel vulnerable and needy, and I don't like it.

As well as the cinema, we go shopping together, take Samson to the park – all sorts of things. Apart from that, if I am out it's with Mum or Dad and sometimes Joe too. All I actually do on my own, with Samson, is simple, familiar, routine journeys – the walk to and from school, sometimes the walk to the station to meet someone, the walk to Madz's house and the walk to the shop at the end of our road.

We'd been talking about extending my reach – learning new routes to new places. It's something I'd mentioned to Dad before, but he got all nervous and said we'd have to get Gina, my guide dog mobility instructor, to teach me and Samson the routes. Madz was going to help me, but now she won't have time. I feel like my world is suddenly a little smaller.

'I'll still be around,' says Madz, putting her hand on mine and squeezing. 'We can still do things.'

I squeeze her hand back. 'I'll be fine. You'll have to tell me every detail of how it's going!'

'Maybe not *every* detail!' she giggles, as the bell rings for first lesson.

Today feels weird. I'm used to the regular routine of my life. In the last few weeks I've had to adjust to Madz spending time with Ollie, and now I have a note to give to a boy I barely know.

Kyle isn't in my form, but I have three lessons with him today – maths, geography and art. I still haven't worked out a way to approach him in class without anyone noticing. I'll have to wait until after; maybe on the way out of a lesson. The corner of the envelope keeps digging into my thigh, reminding me it's there.

4

I don't manage to catch Kyle after Maths or Geography. I must do it today. I got the sense from Charlie that it was urgent, important, and I can't bear the thought of still having the note at home tonight, worrying about it.

I decide I'll go to the resource room to eat my lunch. That's where the students who need extra support go – and I used to go there before I got friendly with Madz. There's people from all year groups. Sometimes I feel like I'm part of two worlds. In the resource room, you never have to explain or justify. People can just be whoever they are. It's a more caring, protected world.

I used to love the break from the challenges of all my lessons, so many students and different rooms to get used to. The dining hall terrified me back in Year 7. Even when I made friends with Madz, it took a lot of coaxing to get me in there. The real world is far more hostile and challenging, but also more interesting, with way more opportunities. I'm used to it now – and having Samson has made it easier too. But today I don't feel up to the challenge.

'Libby! It's Libby!'

I am greeted like a long-lost friend, although unsurprisingly someone is sitting in the seat that I used to consider mine. Also unsurprisingly, the main fuss is over Samson, rather than me. I hear him sniffing as the smells of tuna and cheese and onion crisps waft through the air.

'Can I stroke your dog?'

'Can I?'

'Just keep your lunches out of his reach,' I tell them. 'Or he might think you're offering him a treat.'

'What's his name?'

'Samson.'

'Hi Libby, it's Jenny,' says the learning support teacher. 'How are you getting on? We haven't seen you in here for ages. And how's Samson?'

'He's made a huge difference,' I tell her. 'I feel much more confident now I have him. I just thought I'd pop in and visit you guys.'

I don't want to admit that I'm here because I feel

nervous without Madz. And I'm not exactly sure how I'm getting on, now I have a mission to deliver a note for a boy no one's seen for six months.

'It's nice to have you here,' says Jenny. 'I'm making arrangements for support for your English class theatre trip. I'll let you know when I've got more information.'

'Thanks,' I tell her.

'We've missed you!' says a voice. I have to think for a bit to work out who it is.

'Is that Dylan?' I ask.

'Yes. Had you forgotten me?'

Dylan has Muscular Dystrophy. 'No – but you sound a bit different.'

'His voice has broken,' says Rafique.

'Yeah – I'm a man now, eh?' says Dylan.

'You don't exactly talk like a man,' Rafique teases. 'It's not just the deep voice. It's what you actually say. No offence, mate.'

'None taken,' says Dylan, laughing.

'Libby, come and sit over here and meet Josie,' says Jenny. 'She's in Year 7 and she's losing her sight. I know that's very different, but it might inspire her to see how well you manage.'

'OK,' I say, though I feel awkward. 'Hi Josie.'

'Hi. Your dog is lovely!' Josie's voice sounds young, but without much emotion. 'Are you completely blind?' she continues. 'Do you mind me asking?'

I explain the little that I can see.

'I don't know how you do it,' she comments. 'I've only had sight in one eye for the last two years and now that's going too. I can't imagine life without being able to see at all.'

'It isn't easy,' I tell her, 'and you'll have to adjust. It's different for me because I've never known anything else. But you can still have friends, go out, study, get a job. My mum always tells me the only thing that will limit me is my self-belief. If I really want to do something, then I'll find a way.'

'You're so upbeat,' says Josie. 'I'm glad you came in here. I've been feeling really down.'

'Well, if you ever want to talk, just ask me,' I tell her. 'And maybe think about getting a guide dog. I highly recommend it. Samson's brilliant company as well as my guide. Some people prefer a cane. It's less work, but you can't cuddle a cane when you feel low.'

'Thanks Libby,' says Josie.

After I've eaten my lunch and all eight people in the room have stroked Samson, I get up to leave.

'Thank you,' Jenny says quietly, as I reach the door. 'I think you were just what Josie needed today.'

I feel happy to have been of help to someone else for a change, and I'm glad I came in. Now it's time to help Charlie. And to do that, I have to find Kyle.

'You're really OK about me and Ollie?' Madz asks as we walk to art. 'You've been a bit quiet all day.'

'Just thinking about my project.' I'm keeping Charlie's note a secret for now, like I promised. I do trust Madz, but she might accidentally let something slip to Ollie, and I hate the idea of that.

Madz is doing pottery for her art project so she's in the room next door. I arrange my half-completed painting on the table near the window with the best natural light, along with the flower photo I am painting from and my magnifier. Miss Afia helps me with the paints. I love the smell of the art room — oil paints and turps. Kyle, who is also doing a painting project, usually sits at the back. I look around, trying to place him, but can only see blurred shapes moving around the room.

'There's a space here,' Miss Afia calls to someone. 'Next to Libby. Do try to be on time!'

'D'you need any colours, Libby? I'm just getting some for myself,' comes a voice. It sounds like Kyle. I turn to see the tall blur of him standing by the next table. I nearly fall off my stool. The tables at the back must already be taken because he's late.

This is my moment. I should give him the note. The art room is big — everyone is spread out. No one will notice. But I feel weird: panicky, frozen to the spot.

5

'I like what you've done there,' Kyle says.

He's come nearer without me realising. He's looking over my shoulder at my painting.

'Kyle, wait,' I say, sensing him taking a step away.

'What?' he asks. 'What can I get you?'

I pull the envelope out and hold it, my hand closed around it. 'This is for you,' I tell him quietly. 'Just take it and put it in your pocket. Look at it later. OK?' As I hand it over, I am still full of curiosity about what's in it. I wonder whether Kyle will tell me, or whether I'll never know now that I've handed it over.

I feel him take it. 'Put it away,' I repeat.

'OK – but . . .'

'Don't ask, please! I could do with some brown paint if you don't mind.'

'Sure. Mid brown?'

'Yes, exactly.'

He's gone. I pick up my brush and dip it in the yellow. As I hold it over the paper, I realise my hand is actually shaking. This is ridiculous. It was just a note. It probably said, *Can you lend me twenty quid?* or something like that. But Charlie was so secretive about it, and he made it seem so important . . . Anyway, I've done it now. My role is over. I feel a little deflated.

'Here's the brown. Shall I squeeze some out?' Kyle's back.

'Thanks – just here.'

He squeezes it on to my palette. I keep all the colours in the same order so I can find the one I want.

'Let me know if you need anything else,' he tells me.

He's being very attentive. Is he being kind, or is it because he's curious about the note? Maybe he thinks I wrote it. I hope he doesn't think it's a love note or something.

I hold the photograph I'm painting from close to my eyes. It's a yellow rose, but it's amazing how many colours there are in it: shades of yellow, but also greens, whites, creams, browns. I look through the magnifier at what I've painted so far.

I love painting. It takes my full focus and there's something so relaxing about it. I love photography even more – macro photography, because I can look through the lens and see so clearly, every tiny detail. It's so different from just looking around me at vague blurred shapes. I'm sure people give me funny looks when they see me out with my camera and a guide dog. Sometimes I hear comments, but I don't let it bother me. So many people think 'blind' just means you can't see. They don't realise how many variations of visual impairment there are.

I need clean water, and pass Kyle's table as I go to get it. I realise I have no idea what his project is. I'm suddenly curious about what he's painting.

'Can I look?' I ask him. 'With my magnifier?'

'Yes, if you want.' He sounds surprised – but pleased too. 'It's not a patch on yours though.'

'I'll just get my water first,' I tell him.

'Shall I do it?' he asks.

'No – it's OK.' I'm touched he is being so sweet, but I like to do things for myself. I keep on a straight path towards the side of the classroom where the sinks are, feel for the edge of the sink and then find the tap. I turn it, listen to water splashing and check with a finger that the pot is not getting too full. I need to be able to carry it back without spilling it.

Kyle's height is a useful landmark as I work my way back to my table. I'm determined not to make a fool of myself by spilling water everywhere now. I feel for the table edge and put the water down carefully, then find and lift my magnifier, taking it back towards Kyle.

'Let me help,' he says, taking it from me and positioning it over his picture.

I look down. Kyle is painting what looks like a fantasy battle scene from a film – monsters with weapons raised, mouths bared with teeth showing.

'Wow! That's intense!' I say, hoping he doesn't take it as an insult. 'I mean – the detail is incredible.'

'I love creating monsters,' he tells me. 'I've not got the perspective right though.'

'I can't tell,' I say honestly. 'Thanks for showing me. I'd better get back to mine.'

After art I have French. Madz is doing German, so at the end of the day I walk with Samson towards the cloakrooms where we usually meet.

'Hey, Libby!' Someone touches the top of my arm gently. 'Libby, it's Kyle.'

'Samson, stand,' I tell him. He stops.

'Listen – that note . . .' says Kyle. 'Can I talk to you for a moment?'

I'm instantly curious, but I don't want to be late.

'Madz will be waiting for me,' I tell him.

'Please, just for a sec,' he says.

'OK.' I tell Samson to turn left and we follow Kyle to a quiet spot round by the old disused lockers.

'Have you read it?' I ask him.

'Yes,' he says. 'Did Charlie give it to you himself? I need to know.'

'Yes,' I say awkwardly. 'What . . . what did it say? Or can't you tell me?'

'It says he needs help.'

'What kind of help?'

'It's bad, Libby.' Kyle's voice is low and serious. 'He thinks someone's going to kill him.'

I'm so shocked, I open my mouth, but can't speak. I feel like I've swallowed a stone. I don't know what I was expecting, but it wasn't that.

Finally, I manage one word. '*What?*'

'I know,' says Kyle. 'My feelings exactly.'

'So what does he want you to do?'

'He wants me to meet him tomorrow. He's told me where. I don't know what to do. I mean, what if I don't go, and then it happens – he gets killed? I'll have to go, won't I? I mean – what do you think?'

'Maybe you should go to the police?' I suggest.

'The note says clearly, "no police",' says Kyle. 'I guess it could put him in even more danger if whoever's after him gets wind that he put the police on to them. If he's asking me to help, he must think there's something I can do.'

'I guess,' I say.

'The note says I'm not to tell anyone,' says Kyle. 'But he must trust you, as he gave you the note. He must've known you'd want to know what was in it.'

I'm not sure that's true, but I don't say anything.

'I think I'll go,' Kyle continues, 'but listen. I want you to memorise the address before I tear it up, so that someone knows where I am. Just in case something happens.'

'What do you think's going on?' I ask him.

'I've no idea. I'm not sure I even want to know,' says Kyle.

I wonder if this is true. Why has Charlie asked

Kyle? Why does he think Kyle can help?

'Maybe I should come with you?' I suggest.

'That's nice of you, but he asked me,' says Kyle. 'And don't get me wrong, but you and Samson . . . you're a bit conspicuous. No – I'll go alone.'

'I'll give you my number,' I suggest. 'Then you can call me and let me know what happens.'

'OK,' he says. 'Thanks for letting me talk to you about it. See you tomorrow.'

'Were you talking to *Kyle*?' Madz asks, as I approach the cloakroom.

One problem with not being able to see much is that I never know who's watching me.

'Were you spying on me?' I tease.

'Just came to see where you'd got to,' she says. 'Why? Is something going on with you two?'

'Of course not! We were talking about our art projects.'

'And you had to go off by yourselves to do that?' she asks, clearly not believing me.

'So we could hear each other and so I didn't get knocked about by everyone getting their stuff,' I say gruffly.

'I think he likes you,' she tells me. 'I saw the way he was looking at you.'

'How?' I ask.

'All intense, like,' says Madz.

'Really? Well he's going to be disappointed then.'

'You don't like him?'

'It's not that,' I tell her.

Madz is so lovestruck that she has a one-track mind, while I know any intense look was because Kyle's worried about Charlie's note. But I can't explain that to Madz.

'He's good-looking,' she comments, 'but he's a bit brooding. You never quite know what's going on in his head.'

'You never know what's going on in anyone's head,' I point out. 'Someone can act like they're really happy when they're a mess inside.'

'True,' says Madz.

'Kyle's got a nice voice,' I comment.

'So you *do* like him!' she exclaims.

'Can we talk about something else?' I beg, laughing.

6

At the time Kyle should be meeting Charlie, I'm trying to concentrate on my maths homework, but failing. It's frustrating – maths is one of my best subjects. I keep stopping and checking my phone for messages, though I know it will beep if one comes. I barely know Kyle and I've not thought about Charlie in the last six months, yet I feel anxious. I pause and lean down to stroke Samson, who's lying by my feet next to the desk.

Finally, I get so fed up with waiting that I text Kyle using Voiceover, which translates my voice into text and reads texts out to me. 'Did you meet?'

There's no reply.

It's not until I'm getting ready for bed that a message comes through.

'He wasn't there.'

My phone speaks the words of Kyle's message aloud. I had been imagining all sorts of things: Charlie running for his life, someone after him, wanting Kyle to hide him somewhere or wanting money to pay someone off. Somehow I never thought that he might not show at all.

'No way!' I reply.

'I waited for two hours – just in case.'

'Two hours!'

'Can we meet? I'm not sure what to do.'

I feel immediately pleased, and then knock myself for feeling it. Surely it would be better if Kyle had met Charlie, sorted out whatever it was, and it was over? I don't want to get involved – or do I? I can't help feeling worried about Charlie, and I feel sorry for Kyle. He didn't ask to be involved either. But maybe we can help Charlie together.

'OK,' I text back. Am I actually arranging to meet a boy? This feels weird.

'Tomorrow morning? Where's good for you?'

I'm glad he's asking, as it needs to be somewhere I know. 'How about the park? By the Roman Street gate?' I suggest. Samson loves it there so at least he'll get a walk too.

'Great. Around 11am?'

'Fine.'

*

Saturday breakfast is one of the few times we're all together as a family. We all like a lie-in on a Saturday so it is more of a brunch really, at about ten.

Today we're having pancakes. I've made the batter with Dad's guidance – he's the pancake expert – and Joe is responsible for tossing them.

'Is something up, Libby?' Mum asks.

Considering she's not around as much as Dad, Mum can be very perceptive. Sometimes I wish she wasn't.

'Just a crazy week,' I tell her. 'Madz has been busy so I'm doing more without her. I'm getting around the school more on my own.'

'You're doing so well,' says Mum.

'She certainly is,' Dad agrees.

'Keep challenging yourself,' says Mum. 'You and Samson will be charging all over town on your own before you know it.'

'Steady on,' says Dad. 'There's no need to rush things. In your own time, Libby.'

Mum doesn't answer, but I can tell she's irritated.

'I'm going to take Samson to the park this morning,' I tell them. 'I'll do some more homework this afternoon.'

Samson huffs with delight at the word *park* and wags his tail against my legs. The smell of pancake batter cooking wafts around the room and my stomach rumbles.

'And what are you up to today, Joe?' Mum asks.

'What?' says Joe. 'Oh, Mum! Now I've dropped one. That's you, distracting me! Oh . . . Samson! Libby!'

'What?' I say.

'He's wolfed it down already.'

'He ate the pancake you dropped?' I ask.

'Yes – he was so fast.' Joe laughs. Mum and Dad are laughing too.

'Oh Samson!' I exclaim. 'I think he thought you dropped it there specially for him,' I tell Joe. 'At least it saves you cleaning up.'

'Right. This next one's for you, Libby,' says Joe.

'Don't talk to Joe, Mum,' I warn. 'I don't want you distracting him again.'

It's a lovely day, but I feel suddenly nervous as Samson guides me eagerly towards the park. This is one of the routes we practised with Gina, my guide dog mobility instructor, when I first got Samson, so we're very familiar with it. I'm deliberately a couple of minutes late in the hope that Kyle will be waiting for me, but he isn't there yet. I stand by the gate and tell Samson to sit. Doubts start to rattle through my head. Maybe this wasn't a good idea.

'Excuse me,' someone says, making me jump. 'Do you need any help?'

'I'm fine. Thanks for asking,' I reply.

When someone sees me standing still, alone with Samson, they seem to think I must need help. At least this person asked politely. Sometimes people grab my arm and try to take me across a road that I don't even want to cross.

'Hi Libby!'

I'm so relieved that Kyle is here.

'Hi you!' I say.

'And hi Samson,' says Kyle. 'Shall we walk? Do you . . . do you need me to help you or do anything? You'll have to tell me. I just don't want to do the wrong thing . . .'

'I'm fine. I know the park well and Samson can guide me,' I say.

The path around the park is as familiar as an old friend, so I don't need to concentrate much. I'm relieved at last to be able to talk about everything that's been going round in my head.

'What do you think's going on with Charlie?' I ask. 'I can't believe he didn't show.'

'Me neither,' Kyle says as we walk towards the lake. 'I'm really worried. He says someone wants to kill him and he doesn't show. What am I meant to think?'

'You're not . . . you're not saying it's already happened?' I say, swallowing. I don't want to use the word 'dead'. I don't even want to think it. 'I mean, it would have been on the news or something, wouldn't it?'

'Only if . . . if he was found.' He pauses. I find I'm holding my breath. 'But it isn't likely,' Kyle continues. My breath flows once again with relief. 'Maybe it just wasn't safe for him, so he stayed away.'

'Should we go to the police?' I wonder aloud.

'He said no police, remember,' says Kyle.

'You're right,' I say. 'We don't want to put him in more danger. But what else can we do?'

'I'm glad you're saying *we*, Libby. I feel kind of scared, and it's good I can talk to you about all this.'

'I feel the same,' I tell him – and I get this slight

fluttering feeling in my tummy. 'Can we sit down on a bench?' I suggest. 'Then I can take Samson's harness off and he can have a run around.'

'There's a bench,' says Kyle. 'Do I need to watch him? How do you know where he is?'

'He's trained not to go far – and he has a bell so I can hear him too,' I explain. 'It'd still be good if you can keep an eye out. I prefer to know someone can see him.'

'Sure thing,' says Kyle.

'Off you go, Samson!' I tell him, once we're sat down. He nuzzles me gratefully and then he's gone. I breathe in the smell of newly mown grass and listen, aware of the distant laughter of children in the playground where Joe and I used to go when we were younger, and the cheerful birdsong in the trees close by.

'He's having a sniff in the bushes,' Kyle tells me. 'His tail's wagging – he looks very happy.'

'Good,' I say. 'What do you know about Charlie, Kyle? Do you have any idea what he's been up to since he stopped coming to school?'

'I haven't a clue,' he says. 'I heard Kajun and Raf talking about him a while back, and they said it was like he'd disappeared off the face of the planet. He used to hang out with them sometimes, so if they didn't know anything . . .'

'Didn't you hang out with him at all?' I ask.

'No.'

'Why do you think he asked you, then?' I comment. 'If you weren't even friends?'

I hear Kyle sigh. 'We're not friends, but we went to the same primary school. We hung out sometimes there. He was cheeky in class. We had a laugh. He changed so much. He wasn't so angry then.'

'But you want to help him now? Why?' I ask.

Kyle speaks quietly. His voice has a dreamy tone. 'He did something for me once. I feel I kind of owe him.'

I'm curious now. 'What did he do?'

There's such a long pause I wonder if Kyle heard me. I'm about to ask again when Kyle says, 'He saved my life.'

7

'Saved your life?' This is so big, so unexpected. I feel a strange kind of dizziness. The bright sun isn't helping. I hold my hand in front of my face. 'What happened?'

'It was years ago, when we were ten,' says Kyle. 'We got abducted by a man in a car.'

I feel that stone again, the one I felt like I swallowed yesterday, and it's lying heavy in in my tummy. I'm scared of what he's going to say next. I move my hand from shielding my eyes, putting it over my stomach instead. 'What happened?'

'Sometimes we walked home from school together. It was raining the day it happened and we were drenched. We weren't even wearing coats. This car stopped and a man wound down the window.'

Kyle's voice has lost all expression. I sense this is hard for him to talk about.

'Go on,' I tell him.

'The man – he smiled at us and said something like, "I thought it was you! You look like drowned rats! Here, get in, I'll give you a lift." I reckoned it must be someone Charlie knew,' Kyle explains. 'Charlie thought the same. He said after, he thought I knew the guy. Anyway, we both just got in. He started driving. He didn't ask where we lived, so again, we both thought he knew already. It was raining so hard, we could hardly see out the windows. But he turned the wrong way at the traffic lights. That's when I panicked.'

'So Charlie didn't know him either?' I say, in horror.

'Exactly,' says Kyle.

I'm trying to imagine this. I can only relate it to the feeling I've had when I'm out alone and a stranger grabs my arm, without saying anything first. They might be trying to help, but in that moment I don't know that – they might be intending to steal my bag or phone or pull me into the bushes. That's scary enough. But this sounds scarier.

'I told the man I thought he'd taken the wrong turn,' Kyle continues. 'My voice was all wobbly. I was just hoping desperately that it was true, he'd made a mistake. He said there were roadworks, but I was sure there weren't any near us.

'I asked him, "Are we going to Charlie's or mine?" But he didn't answer – he said maybe we'd both like an ice cream first. My heart was beating so fast. This wasn't right. It just wasn't. Charlie told the man that was nice of him, but his mum would want him home and I said, me too. Of course, we didn't have mobile phones.

'But the guy questioned why we didn't like ice cream. I was terrified. I couldn't speak any more. Charlie just said, "Maybe another time?"

'Then he said he'd got chocolate biscuits and that no boy could say no to that. I was trying not to piss myself. We'd been warned about getting into cars with strangers. We'd seen the news stories. This man had got us on purpose. He was going to do bad things to us – and then he was going to kill us.'

'So what happened?' I ask, wondering if I even really wanted to know.

'Then the car came to a stop,' says Kyle. 'The man was taking off his seatbelt. I was still paralysed, but Charlie moved so fast. He got the back door open – grabbed me and dragged me out and pulled me and we were running and I'd never run so fast in my life. We didn't look back, not for ages. We were sure he was coming after us. But when we stopped, there was no sign of him. I'd never have got out on my own. Charlie saved me. He got me out.'

'So did you go to the police?' I ask. 'Did they get him?'

'No. Looking back, maybe we should've done. But we didn't even tell our parents. I mean, we'd been stupid, hadn't we? We'd have got a right telling off, both of us. We were OK. We'd learned our lesson. The man was long gone. There was no point in telling anyone. I've never told a soul until today.'

'Oh Kyle, I'm so sorry.' It sounds lame as I speak the words, but I don't know what else to say. 'Charlie helped me once too. But nothing like that.'

'I know he can be trouble, but he's not all bad,' Kyle says quietly. 'We . . .'

'We've got to help him, haven't we?' I finish Kyle's sentence for him. 'We've got to do something.'

'I want to. But what?' asks Kyle.

My mind is whirring. 'Do you know where he lives?' I ask.

'No. He's moved since primary school. I only

knew his old address.'

'There must be someone who knows more,' I say. 'Someone we can talk to.'

'Hang on,' says Kyle. 'He's got a sister. Maybe she can help.'

'A sister? How old is she?'

'Three years younger,' says Kyle. 'I can picture him picking her up in the playground at primary school and swinging her round and she was laughing. She must be in Year 7.'

'Great!' I say. I feel relieved that there is something we can do. 'Surely she'll know something. Let's find her at school on Monday and ask her.'

'Sounds like a plan,' says Kyle.

I'm about to ask Kyle if he can see Samson, when I hear the jingle of Samson's bell and then panting as he bounds up and rubs his body against my legs. I stroke him gently. 'Good boy, Samson. Let's get the harness back on you. It's time to go.'

'Can I ask you something about Samson?' Kyle says as we start walking back to the gate. 'It may be a stupid question, but I can't help wondering . . .'

'What?' I ask. 'Ask me anything, I won't mind.'

'When Samson poops, how do you know where

he's done it? How do you scoop it up if you can't see? Or don't guide dog owners have to do that?'

I laugh. 'We don't have to, but Samson usually goes in the same place, in our garden, so I know where to scoop. Or if we're out for a long time and we're in a good place for him to go, I can tell him and he'll do it if he needs to – and stay put so that I can find the spot.'

'Clever dog you've got there,' says Kyle. 'You two are so good together. Like proper friends.'

'Yeah. Though I don't go round picking up all my friends' poop, you know,' I joke.

8

On Monday, it doesn't take us long to find Tia, Charlie's sister. The Year 7 girls tend to hang out in the quad, so Kyle and I head there at lunchtime.

'You're Tia Smithson, aren't you? Charlie's sister?' I hear Kyle say.

'Who are you?'

'Kyle. You probably don't remember me. I used to walk to school with Charlie sometimes when we were at primary.'

'No, you're right. I don't remember you,' she says abruptly. 'What d'you want?'

'We're looking for Charlie,' I tell her.

'Why?' There's a suspicious tone to her voice.

'Do you know where he is?' Kyle asks, ignoring her question.

'I might. I asked you why you're looking for him.' Her voice is defiant, but young. I'd take her for nine or ten, though she must be eleven or twelve.

'Is he OK?' I ask. 'We were just worried. He was in our form group, and it's ages since he's been at school.'

'Yeah, six months. And *now* you worry?'

'Is he at home?' Kyle asks.

'No,' she replies. 'I haven't seen him for ages. But I do know where he is. So why should I tell you anything?'

'I'll be honest with you,' I tell her softly. 'We've heard he's in trouble – in danger. We don't want anything to happen to him. Maybe you could just check on him and let us know?'

'*Me?*' Tia sounds stunned. 'You want *me* to go checking up on him?'

'Don't you care about him?' I ask. 'He's your brother. If my brother was in danger, I'd want to check on him.'

'Look,' she says. 'Oh – sorry – I shouldn't say that, should I? You can't.' She sniggers. She's mocking me and I don't like it. But I put up with it as I want information.

Kyle has other ideas. 'Whoa, Tia . . .' he says, jumping in to defend me, which is rather sweet.

'It doesn't matter,' I say.

Tia pauses, then says, 'Sorry. I don't want to be mean to you because I know you can't see. But you *don't* see. You don't get it, you don't know what he's like. I'm glad he's gone. Life's better without him. And you're right, I don't care. He'd changed. He never spoke to me any more, you know? Not a word – not an answer to a question. When he bothered to come home, he shut himself away in his room. And I reckon he was stealing 'cos he was buying stuff, and Dad's asking him, "Where d'you get the money for that?" and he just swore at him – and Mum too. That's not the way you treat people you care about, is it? So why should I care about him?'

'If you don't care about Charlie,' says Kyle, 'then why do you care about telling us where he is? Why does it matter?'

She's quiet now. Then she sighs. 'You really want to find him that much?' she says. 'I'll tell you then, just to get rid of you. If you're trouble for him, so what? He's staying at our nan's. I'll give you the address. You got a pen? I'll write it down. Just don't tell him I told you, OK?'

'Thank you so much,' I tell her.

'You don't have to thank me. Just leave me alone.'

'Come on Libby,' says Kyle, once Tia's written the address and given it to him. 'Let's get some lunch.'

Kyle actually wants to eat lunch with me? I'm relieved, as I know Madz is eating with Ollie. I follow him towards the dining hall and he even offers to carry my tray.

Once we're sitting down and eating, I say, 'She was unbelievable! She couldn't care less about her own brother.'

'It's sad,' says Kyle.

I feel a pang, remembering what Kyle said about Charlie swinging his sister round in the playground. It makes me think about my relationship with Joe. We never played or laughed much together when we were younger and I've never felt close to him, though I don't know why exactly. I always felt he was jealous that I got more attention because I couldn't see. But it wasn't my fault.

'Where does Charlie's nan live?' I ask.

'In Golton,' says Kyle. 'About twenty minutes on the bus. We could go there after school.'

That 'we' gives me a warm feeling inside. Kyle and I are going to go together to find Charlie.

'Oh, but only if you want to,' he adds. 'I

thought . . . I mean, you don't have to . . .'

'I do want to come,' I say. But now I have a tingly feeling in my legs. The thought of getting on a bus and going off somewhere strange – and with a boy I barely know – feels scary. I usually like to know exactly what I'm doing, have everything planned out so that I feel safe. But I'm also excited. For me, this feels like a real adventure.

'I'll just have to let my gran know I'll be late home,' I tell him.

'Great,' he says.

I walk beside Kyle with Samson slightly ahead on his harness. My heart's beating faster than usual, but I'm trying to act like this is a normal, everyday thing to do. I texted Gran to say I'm staying late to get some help with homework. I've never lied to Gran before, and I don't want to think about it or I'll feel guilty. Samson dutifully stops when we reach the corner and I ask Kyle which way to turn.

'I thought Samson guides you,' he comments.

'I have to tell him where to go,' I explain. 'He'll stop at the kerb and move round cars parked on the pavement. He's even trained to watch for low hanging branches, but he doesn't know which way to go unless I tell him.'

'I never realised that,' says Kyle. 'Do you – do you want to take my hand? If it would help, I mean.' He sounds really awkward, but so sweet with it.

'Thanks. But I'm OK with Samson guiding. If I do need your help, it's better if I hold on to your arm, just above the elbow.'

'Maybe we can try that some time,' says Kyle. 'It's left here.'

'Samson, left,' I tell Samson, and he dutifully turns. We walk on without talking, but that suits me as I need to concentrate when it's not a familiar route.

'We can cross here,' says Kyle, when we reach the road. His shape steps out beside me, but Samson stops abruptly and won't cross.

'Kyle! Wait!' I say.

'What's wrong? There's nothing coming.' Kyle steps back on to the kerb. 'I did look both ways, you know.'

'Is there a crossing?' I ask.

'Yes, down there. But it's safe to cross here, I promise.'

'If Samson can see a crossing, he won't let me

55

cross here where it's less safe,' I explain. 'He's been trained to cross at crossings, if there is one.'

'What's Samson doing now?' Kyle asks when we reach the crossing.

'Showing me where the button is to press — pointing with his nose,' I explain. 'Under here, there's a cone that spins when the green man appears, so someone who can't see well knows it's safe to cross.'

Samson stops again.

'He's sniffing the air,' Kyle tells me.

I sniff too. 'Is it McDonalds?' I ask.

'You're right!' Kyle laughs. 'He likes McDonalds, does he?'

'Yes! He likes the smells in there.' I bend down to Samson. 'No, Samson, not today!' I tell him. 'Forward!'

The bus pulls up as we reach the bus stop so we don't have to wait. I don't often go on buses and I'm worried it will start moving before I've sat down.

'There's two seats near the back,' says Kyle, but Samson is already guiding me down the bus and puts his head on a seat so I can find it. Kyle sits down next to me and Samson snuggles in close by my feet as the bus pulls away. I slide towards Kyle as the bus jolts and pull back awkwardly, feeling for the pole, so I can hold on.

'What if no one's home when we get to Charlie's nan's?' I ask.

'It'll have been a wasted journey,' says Kyle. 'But we've got to try.'

Kyle's quiet on the bus. I listen in on someone else's conversation about the weather and how long this hot spell will last. It's much hotter than usual for June. I check my watch, and we've been on the bus for twenty-five minutes.

'Are we nearly there?' I ask.

'I think it's the next stop.'

I tell Samson and he's up and ready to guide me off the bus when it stops. I'm more self-conscious than usual, not wanting to make a fool of myself in front of Kyle by tripping down the step.

'It's just down this road, according to Google Maps,' Kyle tells me.

'Forward,' I tell Samson. The road is narrow with cars parked half on the pavement, so Kyle walks in front and Samson carefully guides me round.

'This is the house. I'm ringing the bell,' Kyle tells me.

'Sit, Samson,' I tell him and he obeys. We wait. I wonder who will answer the door. What if it's Charlie? What will he say when he sees me? But nothing happens. I'm starting to think no one is there at all when I hear the door click open.

'You collecting for Guide Dogs for the Blind?' a woman's voice asks. She's shorter than me and her voice is soft, kind. 'I'm sure I have a few spare coins somewhere. Hold on . . .'

'We're not collecting for charity,' I say. 'We're looking for Charlie.'

'*Charlie?*' Her surprise is clear as her voice goes high. 'Well you won't find him here.'

'We heard he was staying with you,' Kyle says.

'He was.'

'But not any more?' I ask.

'No.' She sighs. 'You friends of his? He's never mentioned a blind friend . . . Don't get me wrong – I love that boy to bits – but there was only so much his poor old nan could put up with.'

'What happened?' I ask.

'You must know what he's like. I never knew whether he was coming or going. He was out all hours of the night. He worried me silly. Rude too, he was.

58

No respect. I told him he had to change his ways. But he didn't. In the end I told him to go home, sort things out with his parents. It was only ever meant to be a short-term thing, staying with me. And would you believe he raided my purse before he left!'

'But he hasn't gone home,' I tell her. 'Tia told us he was here.'

'Not at home? Well, he hasn't been here for a month or more,' she says. 'My son Vince – Charlie's dad – he and I aren't really on speaking terms. I never heard from him. I just assumed . . .'

'Can you think of anywhere else Charlie could've gone?' I ask.

'Who knows?' she says. 'I despair of that boy. I tried my best, I really did. Let me think . . . There's no one else in the family who'd have taken him. I don't know who he was mixing with, apart from the one mate I sometimes overheard him talking to on the phone. Hassan – that was his name. I think he met him at that unit he was at for a time. I can't think where he'd have gone.'

Charlie's nan has been nattering on and yet we're no closer to finding him. At least Hassan is a lead. 'Do you know where Hassan lives?' I ask.

'Not a clue,' she says.

'Thanks for talking to us,' I tell her.

'No problem – and I'm sorry I thought you were collecting. I do always give to Guide Dogs for the Blind, you know. He's a lovely one you've got there.'

9

'What do we do now?' asks Kyle, as we walk back to the bus stop.

'What was that unit she mentioned?' I ask. 'Was that the one Charlie got sent to when he was excluded?'

'Yes,' says Kyle. 'I know the one, it's in Canley Road. Near the library. I've walked past it.'

'We could go there, I guess,' I suggest. 'See if anyone knows where we can find Hassan?'

'It's too late to go now,' says Kyle. 'We could go after school tomorrow.'

I hesitate, wondering what I'd tell Gran. I'd need to make up another excuse, and she might get suspicious. I also have homework to do.

'It's OK if you don't want to come,' says Kyle. 'I can go on my own.'

'I do want to help,' I explain, 'but I need to do my homework too.'

'Why don't I go to the unit tomorrow on my own and I'll text and let you know if I find out anything?'

'Yes,' I say gratefully. 'Please do let me know. It's not that I don't care.'

'I know that, don't worry,' he says. 'I'm glad you came with me today.'

When we reach the bus stop, it's a longer wait for the bus this time and I'm relieved to get on it. Samson climbs on eagerly, also clearly glad to head for home.

There's a seat here, Libby,' Kyle says, guiding my hand gently towards it. He's learning fast, and has a good instinct for how to help me. I'm surprised how safe I feel with him. He's quiet again on the journey though, and I try to think of questions to ask so he'll talk. I'm used to travelling with Madz, who never stops talking.

'Do you have any brothers or sisters?' I ask.

'No. It's just me. Me and my mum.'

'Must be quiet in your house,' I joke.

'Quieter than you'd think,' he comments. 'My mum's not well. She can't get out much and she gets depressed. I sometimes get worried and stay home to be with her. That's why I skip school now and then. She can go days and days barely saying a word.'

'Oh – that's rough,' I say. 'Sounds lonely.'

'Yeah. What about you?'

I tell him about Joe and his reptiles, and manage to get a laugh out of him when I tell him how I once found a lizard asleep on the pillow next to my head.

I'm surprised to find Gran still at home when I get back.

'Your dad's got a meeting,' she tells me, 'and your mum's working late as usual. Where've you been, Libby? I know you said you'd be late, but I didn't think you meant this late.'

'Went to a friend's,' I tell her. 'We're working together on a project.'

'And how's it going?'

'Bit slow, but we're getting there,' I say, and then to change the subject away from what I'm up to, I ask, 'How are things with Dominic? Have you seen him again?'

'Oh yes, and he's invited me to go to the theatre on Thursday. But it's a matinee, so I wouldn't be here when you and Joe get home.'

'Oh Gran – you must go,' I say. 'Joe and I will be fine.'

'Maybe I will,' says Gran. 'I must admit, I'd love to. I'll see what your dad thinks about it when he gets home later.'

Unsurprisingly, Dad's not completely sure about leaving us unsupervised without Gran.

'Dad, we'll be fine,' I assure him – and Joe surprises me by speaking up and agreeing.

'We will, Dad,' he says.

'We need to let Gran have a life too,' I add.

'You're right – she's not been to the theatre for ages,' says Dad. 'But please be sensible, both of you.'

I'm working hard on my English homework the next day when Kyle calls.

'I hung about outside for a bit,' Kyle tells me, 'and kids started coming out. I saw this girl around our age, and I asked her if she knew Hassan. She said, "Yeah – he's in my group. But he only comes here Thursdays now. You should catch him if you come this time tomorrow." I couldn't believe it.'

'I should be able to come with you tomorrow,' I say eagerly. 'My gran's going to the theatre so I won't have to make up excuses.'

'Great,' says Kyle.

*

Once Dad's gone in the morning, I let Joe know that I won't be straight home after school. He doesn't even ask me why. That's the good thing about Joe not saying much.

The unit is a fifteen-minute walk from school, but it's so hot out, I start to wish I hadn't said I'd go. I've had to put special cream under Samson's paws so the pavement doesn't burn them. I carry a bottle of water and a folding bowl and make sure I give him frequent drinks. Poor Samson. He doesn't protest, but I'm sure he'd rather be lying in the garden in the shade from the apple tree than walking the streets.

'I hope that girl was right and Hassan's there today,' I say.

'We're coming up to it now,' says Kyle. 'Oh – and I can see the girl from yesterday. Wait here and I'll go and speak to her.'

I tell Samson to sit and hope Kyle won't be long. He isn't. He's back in a moment. 'Hassan's still in there – she's gone to get him.'

'Hi. I'm Hassan.' The shape of the person in front of me is a bit shorter than Kyle but not by much. His voice is deeper. 'Ruby said you were looking for me?'

'Hi,' I say. 'We're actually looking for Charlie. Charlie Smithson. His nan thought he might be staying with you.'

'I haven't seen him for a couple of weeks,' says Hassan.

'Do you know where he is?' I ask. 'We're worried about him.'

'I'd help you if I could, but I'm not sure what I can tell you,' says Hassan.

'Man, it's hot. Let's go and get a cold drink,' Kyle suggests.

'You're right,' says Hassan. 'When's it going to cool down?'

'We could go to that café over there?' says Kyle.

I sense doubt in Hassan's lack of response and his blurry shape moves back. 'I dunno,' he says. 'I don't want to miss my bus. But I've got twenty minutes, I guess . . . Come on then.'

'Great,' says Kyle. 'There's a table over there in the shade.'

'Samson, forward,' I say, and Samson follows Kyle. I'm glad to sit down out of the sun.

'What would you like?' asks Kyle.

'A slushie,' I tell him.

He laughs. 'I was asking Hassan, actually. But no worries, of course I'll get you one.'

'Oh — sorry.' I'm embarrassed when things like this happen, thinking someone's speaking to me when they're talking to someone else.

'I'll have an iced coffee,' says Hassan. 'Ta.'

I'm left with Hassan while Kyle goes for the drinks and I'm not sure what to say.

'How do you know Charlie?' he asks.

'He was at our school,' I explain. 'How about you? Did you meet him here at the unit?'

'Yes.'

'So did you get excluded from school too, like Charlie?' I ask. 'I mean — I hope you don't mind me asking . . .'

'I don't mind, but you're wrong there, as it happens,' Hassan says. 'It wasn't like that for me.'

'I shouldn't have assumed,' I say quickly. 'Sorry.'

'I was getting bullied at school, really badly. My school was rubbish. They did nothing about it. I started refusing to go,' Hassan explains. 'Then they offered me a place here. It's a bit weird when you think about it, as some of the other kids have been excluded for doing the bullying. But they're not so bad, most of them. It's a nice small group and the teacher's great – he can handle anything. I'm getting on OK. I've started at a different school part-time now.'

'Here you go,' says Kyle, returning with the drinks. 'This is yours, Libby.' I reach out gingerly and he pushes the cup towards my hand.

'Thank you,' I say. I take a sip and the icy slush cools my mouth. 'So, Hassan, do you have any idea where Charlie could be? His nan told us you're friends with him.'

'Not exactly friends,' says Hassan. 'We hung out together at the unit a bit, and then when things went belly-up for him at his nan's he said he needed somewhere to stay for a few days. I felt sorry for him, so he came to ours. I should have asked my mum and dad first. They weren't too pleased, but they put up with him for a week. Then they said he had to go.'

'So where did he go?' I ask.

'He said he'd be on the streets, but I didn't think he meant it. I said he should go home. I knew it wouldn't be easy after what his dad told him, but still, his parents wouldn't want him sleeping rough, I'm sure. But I'm guessing he isn't there.'

'No, he isn't,' Kyle tells Hassan.

'His dad?' I ask. 'What did his dad tell him?'

'That he wasn't Charlie's real dad. He just came out with it, like that. They were having a row, Charlie said – and his dad suddenly yelled, "Thank God you're not really my son!"'

Kyle gives a sharp outbreath. 'Whoa. That must've been a shock.'

'Horrible,' I agree, trying to imagine what it would feel like to hear something like that.

'Yeah – he took it hard. And not surprising,' says Hassan.

'I don't think his sister knows. Or his nan,' I comment, thinking aloud. 'They were just complaining about him stealing money and staying out late.'

'I told him to keep in touch,' says Hassan, 'but I think he felt I'd let him down – that I should have been able to convince my parents to let him stay. I haven't heard from him since he left. I texted him but he never replied.'

'It's not your fault,' I tell him. 'It was kind of you to have him stay in the first place. He couldn't expect your family to take him in long-term.'

'He might be sleeping rough now though,' says Kyle. 'It sounds like he ran out of options. There's an arch not far from the station where some people sleep, and also on benches in the park, or doorways along Ferren Street. We could try there.'

'I'm sorry I didn't help Charlie more,' says Hassan. 'He wasn't a bad guy. I hope you find him.'

'I wish we had a photo of him,' I comment. 'One that we could show people to see if anyone's seen him. We should have asked Tia.'

'I think I've got one on my phone,' says Hassan. 'It's not just him, it's the group of us, larking around at the unit a few months back. Here – you can see him quite well. I can WhatsApp it to you?'

'Thanks – that'd be great,' says Kyle. He gives Hassan his number – and I hear it ping as the photo comes through.

10

'Do you think he really is sleeping rough?' I ask Kyle. I've heard of homelessness of course, but it isn't visible to me.

'Who knows?' says Kyle. 'Let's have a look. We can walk along the high street and then back towards the station.'

'Can you see people now?' I ask him, as we reach the high street. 'How many doorways have people sleeping there?'

'I can't see anyone at the moment,' Kyle says.

'I'm glad,' I say. 'I suddenly worried that people were sleeping outside nearly every door and I've just never known they were there.'

'There's someone sitting near the pub. She's got a sign saying "homeless, please help" and a cup for money.'

'Here – I've got some cash,' I tell him. 'Put a few coins in and ask her about Charlie.'

'Hi,' says Kyle, as we reach her. I hear the jingle of coins as they drop into the cup.

'Thanks,' the woman says quietly. 'Dear girl, looks like you've been cursed to have a difficult life, like me.'

'I don't feel cursed,' I protest.

'I do,' she says grimly. 'At least we both have the companionship of a loyal friend. What's yours called?'

'Kyle,' I say.

'Errm,' says Kyle. 'I think she's referring to Samson, not me. She's got a dog too, tucked up with her. A tiny one.'

'Oh!' I say. 'Sorry – this is Samson. What's your dog called?'

'Rufus,' she says.

Rufus gives a snappy bark and Samson huffs and backs away.

'Actually, we wondered if you could help us,' says Kyle. 'We're looking for a friend who might be sleeping rough. We have a photo. Here . . .'

'Sorry, I don't recognise him,' she says.

'Do you know where else round here we should look?' I ask her.

'Under the arches, maybe?' she suggests. 'You

know – up by the station. Or he could be in a hostel – Jarrins House. I can't stand the place, but some go there, if there's any space. That's up Goddards Street.'

'How long have you been homeless?' I ask her. It may be intrusive to ask, but I'm curious. I've never met someone living like this.

'About eighteen months,' she said. 'But I don't sleep out here, it isn't safe. I'm in a squat.'

I want to ask more, to find out how she ended up like this, but Kyle touches my arm. 'Come on – we'd better keep looking.'

'Yes, of course,' I reply. 'Thank you for talking to us.'

'Hope you find him,' she says.

But we don't.

Kyle says the men under the arches are too drugged up to speak to us. And the one person who is chatty seems to be mentally ill – he's muttering to himself and doesn't even seem to realise we're there.

'What else can we do?' I ask Kyle.

'I don't want to give up yet. We could try that hostel the woman told us about before we go home. What d'you think?'

'It's worth a go,' I say, 'if it's not too far.'

I wait while Kyle finds directions on his phone. 'It's not far at all,' he tells me. 'Come on.'

When we reach Jarrins House we have to buzz an entrance bell, and they don't let us in – they just speak to us through an intercom. Kyle asks about Charlie – Charlie Smithson. The man says he's never come across him, but he could have used a different name to stay there. People often did. We ask to show the photo and he tells us to hold it up to the video-cam. Kyle explains which boy is Charlie.

'He's not familiar. Not at all. Sorry I can't help you.'

We have no choice but to leave. 'I'm not sure he'd have told us even if he did know Charlie,' I say to Kyle as we walk away.

'True – but it's good that they're careful. Charlie asked us for help, but people like that hostel guy aren't to know that, are they? I think Hassan only talked to us because of you.'

'Me? Why?'

'Because you don't look threatening. If it had been just me . . . I'm a teenager, a boy. I could be after Charlie for any reason.'

'But with me,' I intercept, 'you're a boy with a blind friend and a guide dog so you must be a good guy, not a bad one?'

'Yeah, kind of,' says Kyle.

'So is that why you want me to tag along?' I tease. 'I thought you liked me.'

'I do, of course I do!' He laughs. 'It does help though.'

'All those people who sleep on the streets,' I say, 'it makes me grateful that I have a home and a family.'

'Yeah. My life's not always great,' says Kyle, 'but I do have a comfy bed and my mum cares about me.'

We're quiet now. I'm sure we're both thinking about Charlie. Does he have a bed to sleep in tonight? Is he safe?

Maybe it's good news that we haven't found anything. Mum is always saying that 'no news is good news'. She's always upbeat, Mum. Even now, as I get ready for bed, she's humming to herself while she packs for Amsterdam.

'I'll say goodbye now,' she tells me, 'as I'm off at five a.m. tomorrow.'

'I hope it goes well,' I tell her.

'I'm speaking to a thousand people, Libby,' says Mum. 'I don't think I've ever had such a big audience.'

'That's amazing, Mum,' I say. 'Good luck.'

'It's not about luck. It's about effort and determination,' says Mum. 'Don't forget that, Libby. Luck is only the tiniest element, like being in the right place at the right time.'

I laugh. But I'm thinking about Charlie. If he's sleeping on the streets with his life in danger, is that because he didn't put the effort in – or is it just bad luck?

'I know you always put a big effort into everything you do,' says Mum. 'I'm proud of you. I probably don't tell you that often enough.'

'You do, Mum,' I say. 'You do tell me.'

'And your gran's enjoying herself with Dominic,' says Mum. 'It's nice she's found someone to spend time with. I've convinced your dad you don't need her here after school every day and Gran seemed pleased when I told her.'

'Thanks Mum,' I tell her and I give her a hug.

I'm glad about Gran because this will give me much more freedom to help Kyle without awkward questions, but I don't sleep well. I can hear the pitter patter of rain against the window, and then it starts to come down harder, thudding loudly against the glass. Then the thunder and lightning start. Samson barks crossly and I get up and hug him. I'm thinking about all the people sleeping in doorways and under station archways, while I'm lying in my cosy bed. I feel guilty. Any one of them might be Charlie.

I'm half asleep when I go downstairs for breakfast in the morning.

'At least it should be cooler today, after that storm,' Dad says. The radio is on, and I hear the clink of Dad putting his breakfast things in the dishwasher, about to leave for work. As I reach for the bread bin, I bump into the back of a chair – and it's not as if it's even sticking out.

'You sure you're awake?' Dad comments. 'Your mum didn't disturb you when she left, did she?'

'No, but I didn't have a great night,' I tell him.

'That was quite a storm,' Dad says. 'Or is something worrying you? You know you can always talk to me about anything, don't you, Libby?'

'Thanks Dad, but I'm fine. I'm sure it was just the storm.'

As I put some bread in the toaster, the newswoman on the radio reports a stabbing. I listen harder. She's saying a teenage boy has been stabbed to death. I feel a chill through my blood.

'Kids carrying knives . . . it has to stop!' says Dad. 'They think it's for protection, but they've got to realise if they're carrying a knife, they're more likely to either end up dead or in prison for killing someone else.'

I hear him pick up his things and he comes over and kisses me on the head. 'Gotta go. Take care, Libby. Have a good day.' He calls up the stairs. 'Joe, get out of bed, will you? See you later.'

Once Dad's gone, I text Kyle. '**Boy stabbed last night. Did you hear? What if it was Charlie?**'

Samson comes and sticks his nose on my phone. I stroke him gently while I wait for a response. Kyle is probably busy getting ready for school.

'**Not likely,**' he replies. '**I checked online. And a long way away.**' This is followed by about six emojis.

'**Can you stop all the emojis?**' I text back. '**They take ages to audio describe.**'

'**Oh – I never thought of that. Sorry!**'

'**I'm worried,**' I text back. '**Even if it isn't Charlie,** he could be next.'

Then my phone rings. 'You OK?' Kyle asks. He sounds like he really cares and I'm glad we're speaking and not texting.

11

We don't find out the name of the boy who was stabbed until Sunday. It's not Charlie, to my immense relief. I call Kyle.

'I don't know what we can do,' he says. 'We've run out of leads.'

'We could go back to Tia?' I suggest. 'Maybe she knows something that will help, even if she doesn't think she does.'

We look for Tia at school on Monday (well, Kyle does) but frustratingly we don't find her. Then Kyle spots her ahead of us just as we're coming out at home time.

'Can you call her?' I ask him, telling Samson to walk faster.

'She's too far in front. We can follow though, if that's not too creepy? Then we'll see where she lives. Perhaps she'll talk more if she's not got her friends close by.'

We follow for a bit. The cooler spell after the rain only lasted a couple of days, and it's getting much hotter again. We're walking in the opposite direction to my house and I hope we don't have to go too much further. Kyle then tells me the friend she's walking with has said goodbye and gone a different way. 'She's stopped at a house. Oh, wait . . . she's seen us.'

'Tia!' he calls. 'We just wanted to talk to you.'

'She's waiting,' he tells me.

'Good I say. 'Hup hup, Samson.' We hurry to catch her up.

'You've not found that brother of mine, have you?' she asks.

'Sorry, no,' I tell her.

'You don't have to be sorry – it's not me that wants to find him.'

'Can we talk to you?' Kyle asks.

'Why? What's in it for me?' Tia demands.

'We found out something you might want to hear,' I tell her.

'Really?' She sounds doubtful. 'Go on then. You can come in – it's too hot to stand around out here. But just in the kitchen with that dog or my mum'll go mad. And only for a few minutes.'

Samson guides me up the step and through the doorway. We immediately turn right into a room and Kyle guides me to a chair.

'You want a glass of squash?' Tia asks.

'Thanks,' I say. I wasn't expecting her to be so kind as to offer drinks, but I realise I'm parched. I hear the sound of the cupboard doors clanking and glass clinking.

'So,' Tia says, once the glass is in my hand.

'Charlie's not at your nan's any more,' says Kyle. 'She chucked him out.'

Tia laughs. 'Not surprised.'

'He went to stay with a friend after that, but the parents wouldn't let him stay long.'

'We're worried that he might be sleeping rough,' I chip in.

'Then he should come home, shouldn't he?' Tia exclaims. 'No one chucked him out from here. If he's on the streets, that's his choice. He's got a bed here he could be sleeping in. No one's stopping him.'

I feel so sad that Tia can speak like this about her own brother.

'Charlie's friend said he left home because he

had a row with your dad,' I tell her.

'They were always at each other,' says Tia.

'But do you know what the row was about?' I ask. 'The one that made Charlie leave?'

'No,' she says.

'Charlie told his friend Hassan that your dad said he isn't really his dad, and that he was glad about that,' I tell her.

'You what?' says Tia. I can hear from her tone that she's genuinely shocked.

'He's your half-brother,' says Kyle. 'Charlie's got a different dad from you.'

'That's not right,' says Tia. 'If that was true, I'd know about it.'

'So you had no idea?' I ask.

'It isn't true,' she insists.

'Then why would your dad say it?' I ask. 'From what Hassan said, he was so angry with Charlie he just blurted it out. I don't think he meant to tell him.'

Tia's quiet for a moment.

'You OK?' I ask.

'Yeah – I . . . I can't . . . I mean, it does make sense – if that happened, then no wonder Charlie left and hasn't come back. It's a shock to me – it must have been a mega-shock to him.'

At that moment I hear a key in the front door.

'What's this, a party?' says a voice.

'Just some kids from school, Mum,' says Tia. 'They've been looking for Charlie.'

I can see her shape in the doorway.

'We're sorry to bother you. We just wanted to talk to Tia,' I say.

'Is that a dog under the table?' she says. 'Tia, you know I don't like dogs.'

'Sorry – he's my guide dog,' I explain.

'Guide dog?' she exclaims. 'So you're blind? You poor thing.'

'I'm not a poor thing. I just can't see much,' I say, clenching my teeth.

'They told me something, Mum,' says Tia. 'About Charlie. I think you'd better sit down.'

'What's he gone and done now?' she asks. 'Been nicked, has he?'

'No, Mum!' Tia exclaims. 'It's about Dad. Go on – you tell her.'

A chair scrapes across the table and I see the blur of Charlie's mum sit down opposite Tia – as far as possible from Samson. I'm relieved when Kyle starts explaining, as I didn't know how to start. Charlie's mum is quiet while Kyle talks. Not even a gasp or a loud breath.

'Is it true, Mum?' Tia demands, sounding tearful. 'Does Charlie have a different dad?'

Her mum is silent, which makes me think it must be true. Finally she answers softly, 'Yeah.'

'Mum!'

'Sorry, love. I can't believe he told Charlie. He never wanted him to know. Charlie was a few months old when I met your dad. I was in a right state and Vince was so lovely. I thought he'd be off when he found out I had a kid, but he was mad about Charlie and said he didn't mind that he wasn't his. When we got married, he said he wanted to be Charlie's dad properly, so we never told him.'

I see the blur of her shape as she stands up and steps away from the table. 'I need a drink,' she says hoarsely. I hear the fridge open and shut.

'They never got on though, did they?' Tia points out.

'Not once Charlie started getting a mouth on him. Chalk and cheese,' their mum agrees, coming back to sit down.

'So what about his real dad then?' I ask. 'Didn't he want to see Charlie?'

'It was a mistake with him,' their mum sighs. 'When I told him I was pregnant, he wanted us to stay together but it was never going to work. He wasn't my type. So I said no and he scarpered. Never heard from him again. Never got a penny out of him. I was skint until I met Vince.'

'We think Charlie might be trying to find his real dad,' I explain. 'Can you tell us anything? His name, where he might be living?'

'I can tell you his name,' she says, sighing. 'But I doubt that will help you much. It's Johnny Hunter. Must be a million of them out there.'

'At least it's something to go on. Thanks for the drink, Tia,' I say, standing up. Samson is quickly on his feet and guiding me out of the house. Kyle follows.

When we get outside, Kyle instantly googles 'Johnny Hunter' and tells me it gets 91,300,000 results.

'She's right. I don't think the name will be enough to find him,' he sighs.

12

Our leads have dried up and we don't even know if Charlie still wants or needs help. He hasn't tried to make contact again. So there isn't really much we can do right now, unless we keep searching the streets. The thing is, if we're not physically looking for Charlie, there's no real reason to meet up with Kyle. He feels like a friend to me now, but I'm not sure he feels the same. When I don't see or hear from him for a few days, I find I'm missing him — especially now that Madz is so busy with Ollie.

I'm pleased on Thursday when Madz says, 'D'you want to come shopping with me on Saturday?' She tells me she's going out with Ollie in the evening and that she wants to get something new to wear. 'He's seen me in everything I've got. Even that awful red top I hate.'

'Yeah — sure,' I say. 'I could do with a couple of T-shirts.'

*

I'm relieved when I wake up on Saturday, knowing that I'm meeting Madz to go shopping because at least this feels normal. Mum's back too, on a high after her successful talk in Amsterdam, and we have our usual pancake breakfast. Madz knocks for me after lunch. Samson wags his tail as I put his harness on. He likes Madz and is pleased we're going out. He won't be quite so pleased once we hit the shops. Clothes shopping isn't Samson's favourite thing.

'I'll make it up to you afterwards, Samson,' I tell him. 'We'll head to the park later.'

As we walk, Madz talks constantly about Ollie. 'He is awesome,' she tells me. 'It's like, when I'm with him, I feel as if I'm glowing inside – like a disco ball, you know? And he bought me this gorgeous heart-shaped chocolate yesterday! He's so thoughtful. He's taking me out to eat tonight and then we're going to a party. It's a sixth former, Harrison Brady – his eighteenth. Do you know him? It's gonna be a really big party with a band. I've never been to a party like that. What shall I wear, Libby? I don't want to let him down. I want to wow him!'

Although I was keen to go shopping, I'm finding all this talk about what to wear for a party a bit annoying. I can't help feeling it's all a bit trivial. I wonder what Madz would say if she knew that I was worrying about someone whose life might be in danger.

'Well?' she asks, when I don't reply.

'Oh Madz. I've never been to an eighteenth birthday party. I've no idea what you should wear, but I'm sure you'll look amazing.'

'What about this?' She holds out the dress so I can feel it.

'Lots of sequins,' I say. 'Will it be itchy?'

'Itchy?' She laughs. 'I don't care. It's worth the sacrifice if I look incredible.'

She's different from me in this respect. I like to look good, but I want to feel comfortable too. I'd never wear anything if I didn't like the feel of the fabric.

'You want to try it on, then?' I say.

'Yes. It's black with flecks of gold. I think I'll look dead sophisticated in it.'

'I'll snap a photo and then I can zoom in and give you my honest opinion,' I tease.

But the dress doesn't fit so we're back to square one. We browse a few shops, but Madz can't find anything she likes. She pops into the loos and I'm standing outside with Samson, wondering how it would feel if Kyle asked me out and and if I'd get as excited as Madz about what to wear. Someone calls my name – and it isn't Madz. It's a male voice.

'Libby?'

It's not Kyle. For a moment I wonder if it's Charlie, but I know this isn't his voice either. 'Who is this?' I ask.

'Sorry, I should have said. It's Hassan – you know, you came to find me the other day. You were looking for Charlie, right?'

'Oh. Hi.'

'You haven't found him yet, have you?' says Hassan.

'No. We've kind of given up. We don't know where else to look.'

'I just spotted you here so I thought I might as well tell you what I found out, though I don't think it's much use. Well, it was your dog I spotted. Sam, isn't it?'

'Samson,' I correct. 'What is it? Do you know

where Charlie is?' I ask, my heart speeding up.

'Not exactly. And I don't know if this helps at all, but a mate from the unit said he thinks Charlie's living in a place called Harwell Heath. He knows this guy who used to hang around here sometimes. Charlie knew him too. Maybe he's gone to stay with him.'

'Do you have an address?' I ask.

'No, sorry. I think it's a village out in the sticks. And he might not even be there. But I thought you'd want to know.'

'I don't know how we'd find him without an address, but I'm glad you told me,' I reply. 'I'll tell Kyle.'

'Good luck. I hope you find him,' he says.

Then he's gone and Madz is back.

'Who was that?' she says. 'I only left you for a couple of minutes and you're chatting up some good-looking boy?' She laughs.

'He's good-looking, is he?' I say. I'm tempted once more to tell her about Charlie, but I don't know where to start.

'He's tasty all right. So what did he want?'

'He was asking about Samson,' I tell Madz.

'Oh,' says Madz. 'Come on – I spy a dress in this shop window. You don't mind if I try on one more, do you?'

Thank goodness this turns out to be the dress of Madz's dreams. And then, when we finally get to my favourite shop, there's a sale on.

'This is the last one,' I tell Samson, who is reluctant to guide me in. He's definitely had enough. Madz describes various clothes to me until I find a couple of tops to try on.

'What do you think?' I ask Madz, coming out in a top that feels like it's a perfect fit and is a lovely silky fabric. 'Is this navy or green?'

'It's dark green,' she tells me. 'With a diagonal flash of black like a lightning strike. It looks great!'

'How much?' I ask.

'Eight pounds – that's fifty per cent off.'

It's only when I've paid that Madz teases me, saying, 'You can wear that when Kyle asks you out.'

'Let's go,' I say, ignoring her. 'Forward, Samson. Home.'

Samson walks on eagerly when he realises we're heading away from the shopping centre.

Back at home, I fiddle with my key and open the

front door, but I trip before I've taken two steps inside and only stop myself falling by pressing my hands against the wall. I reach down. Joe's shoe.

'Joe!' I yell up the stairs crossly. 'You left your shoes in the middle of the hall!'

'Sorry!' he calls back.

It's frustrating. However hard I try to keep everything in its place, other people forget – especially Joe – and leave stuff all over. I go upstairs with Samson and he lies down in relief on my rug for a snooze. I try on my new top for Mum and she's full of compliments.

'She's got a good eye, that friend of yours. That really suits you.'

Once Mum's gone downstairs, I message Kyle. I'm glad when he calls me straight back. It's nice to hear his voice.

'Harwell Heath? I've never heard of the place,' he says. 'Hang on, I'll google it.'

I stroke Samson gently as I wait for Kyle to speak.

'It's miles away,' says Kyle.

'Maybe he's gone there to hide out,' I suggest. 'If someone really wants to kill him . . .'

'You could be right,' says Kyle, 'though it's not a great secret if Hassan's mate knows about it. Shall we go there? I mean, at least this is something – somewhere we can try.'

In my mind, I want Charlie to be there and I want us to find him. But now Kyle's talking about us actually going, I start to have second thoughts.

'But it's so far – and he might not be there. He might never have been,' I point out. 'And we don't even have an address.'

'I'll understand if you don't want to come. I can go on my own,' says Kyle, 'but I'd much rather go with you.'

'What will we do when we get there?' I ask.

'We've got the photo of Charlie. We can ask in the village shop, or anyone we pass. But Libby, like I said, people are much more likely to help if you're with me.'

'OK, I'll come,' I tell him. 'Shall we go tomorrow?'

'Cool. Let's meet at the station at ten.'

Now I have to think of something to tell Mum and Dad. I'll be out for most of the day. But even though I'm doubtful we'll find Charlie, I'm pleased for an excuse to spend more time with Kyle. And I rarely go to places that are completely new to me, so that's good too.

I search Google Maps and scroll across listening to the place names in the area. I don't recognise any of them. 'Tourist site – Harwell House,' my PC reads aloud. Intrigued, I listen to the description – a stately home with award-winning gardens, rare botanical treats, open to the public from March to October.

My first thought is that this could be my excuse – where I tell my parents I am going. Then at least it won't be a complete lie. And it sounds like a great place to take photographs. Maybe we could go there too. Then I feel selfish. We're going to Harwell Heath to find Charlie, not on a day trip for fun.

But I can't tell my parents that I'm going with Kyle. Even Mum would be worried about me going off on a train to a new place with a boy she knows nothing about and has never met. She trusts Madz and would be happy if I was with her – but I'm not keen to tell an outright lie.

In the end I don't have to. I tell Mum about Harwell House and she seems happy that I'm going further afield and getting more confident on public transport. She doesn't even ask who I'm going with, but assumes it's Madz. I don't think it occurs to her that it might not be.

13

It's a beautiful day, hot but with a welcome breeze, and I feel a sense of freedom as Samson and I walk to meet Kyle at the station.

'Hi Libby. Over here,' Kyle calls as I approach the station. I think about how easily he adapts to my lack of sight. It doesn't seem to make him anxious, like it does with some people. He's happy for me to tell him how to help me, and he remembers. Like now, he's come alongside me so I can take hold of his arm. I have the confidence now to sometimes drop Samson's harness and hold just the lead, so that Samson knows he's not guiding me – and to let Kyle take a turn instead.

We get our tickets and wait ten minutes for the train.

'What did you tell your folks?' he asks once we've found seats and Samson is tucked up by my feet.

I tell him about Harwell House.

'I've never heard of it,' he comments.

'I'd love to go there some time,' I tell him. 'It sounds like a great place to take photos.'

'I guess if we have no luck finding Charlie, it's something to do while we're nearby,' says Kyle.

I'm not sure if he means it or if he's joking, but I'm glad he said it anyway.

'Do you mind if I listen to music?' he asks.

'That's fine,' I say. 'I have a book to listen to. As long as you have an eye out for where we are.'

'Sure, of course, and just nudge me if you want to talk,' he adds.

He shuffles around next to me and I assume he's plugging in his earphones. I do the same. I had wondered what we'd find to talk about for an hour and a half as Kyle's not really the chatty sort, but I feel comfortable listening to my book while we are sitting close enough to touch arms.

I'm absorbed in the other world of my book when Kyle nudges me and says we get off at the next stop.

'It's just been fields and more fields out of the window,' he says. 'We really are in the middle of nowhere.'

I put my headphones and my phone in my bag.

Samson sits up, ready for action.

'Next stop,' I tell him.

We get off the train. It seems to be only a few steps out to the street. As we stand there, I am conscious that the air smells different – fresher, cleaner. And there must be lots of trees because I can hear the birds; far more birds than near home.

'There's a sign for that Harwell House,' Kyle tells me. 'But nothing else.'

'Maybe that's where Charlie's living,' I joke. 'Maybe he found out his real dad is lord of the manor and he came here to find him.'

Kyle laughs. 'Wow! I never thought of that.'

'And maybe he is this lord's first son, and therefore boots the one who has always lived with his dad into second place. Charlie will inherit Harwell House and the second son now gets nothing. That's why the second son wants to kill Charlie,' I improvise.

'What book were you listening to on the train?' Kyle asks, chuckling.

'*Wuthering Heights*, Emily Brontë,' I tell him.

'That makes sense,' says Kyle. 'Why don't we go for a walk about? We can find a village shop or café, show the picture and see if anyone recognises Charlie.'

I take Kyle's arm and tell Samson, 'Straight on.' He walks on enthusiastically.

'Can you describe it to me – what you can see?' I ask Kyle.

'Well, it's a narrow street with lots of small, old-looking terraced houses,' he starts.

'And winding,' I add as we turn yet again.

'The pavement is narrow. I'm walking in the road to make room for you and Samson,' he adds.

'I wondered why you seemed shorter!' I exclaim.

'There's a lot of trees and bushes and now some bigger houses. And I can see a sign up ahead for the high street, so hopefully there will be some shops and signs of life. I haven't seen a soul walking about. Just a few passing cars.'

'We're turning right,' Kyle tells me after a few minutes, and I direct Samson. 'I can see a shop and café and post office all in one. Come on, let's go in.'

A bell tings as he opens the door and holds it for me. Samson guides me up the single step. My arm immediately knocks something off a shelf and I stand still.

'What was that?' I say anxiously. 'I'm sorry!'

'Just a packet of biscuits,' says Kyle. 'I've put them back. It's a bit narrow in here – keep your arms in. There's a woman coming out to the till.'

'Hello,' comes a cheerful voice. 'Can I help you?'

'We're looking for –' Kyle begins.

The woman butts in. 'Harwell House? I get so many in here who've got lost trying to find it. They really need better signs.'

'No, actually,' I say. Her shape has become clearer, so I know I'm facing the right way. 'We're looking for a person. A friend of ours. We've got a photo. We wondered if he's been in here – if you recognise him.'

'Missing, is he?' she asks, with interest. 'I can put a poster up in here if you like.'

'That's kind, but we think he's staying in the village,' I explain.

'This is the photo,' says Kyle. 'It's that boy, on the right.'

'Let me grab my glasses so I can have a proper look,' says the woman.

We wait. I cross my fingers. If this woman doesn't recognise Charlie, I'm not sure what we can do. We can't exactly go knocking door to door.

'Hmm,' she says. 'I can't say I recognise him – but that doesn't mean he hasn't been in here. I'm not great with faces.'

The door tings and I turn. Someone else has come into the shop.

'Hey, Janine,' the shop woman calls. 'You recognise this boy? These lot are trying to find him.'

'Give us a look.' Janine's voice is higher, younger.

I hold my breath.

'I seen 'im!' she announces. 'Down my street, the other end. Sometimes he's with other lads. They're not from round here, none of them. They're good lookers, especially this one. I think it's number five – or could be seven. There's usually a stack of pizza boxes outside. I noticed him 'cos I thought he was kinda cute. I'm sure it's him.'

'Oh – thank you!' I tell her. 'What street? Can you give us directions?'

'Shall I tell the dog?' she asks.

I can tell she's serious. I am speechless, though it isn't the first time someone's tried to tell Samson the way instead of me.

'No,' I say, making an effort to sound calm. 'You

need to tell me — and Kyle — and I will then direct
Samson step by step. He understands forwards, back,
left, right, but not a whole string of instructions.'

'Oh. OK,' she says. She sounds disappointed.

She tells us the way. It's complicated enough for
me, let alone Samson. I hope Kyle's taking it in — and
that Google Maps will help if we get stuck.

We leave the shop and Samson and I follow Kyle
along the narrow pavement, turning this way and
that until I have completely lost my bearings.

'Do you know where we are?' I ask Kyle.

'It shouldn't be much further,' he assures me.

We walk on, past a post box, and the pavement
gets more uneven.

'Careful,' says Kyle. 'The tree roots here have
pushed the paving stones up.'

I take small steps until he comes to a stop. 'This is
number five — and there are pizza boxes like that
woman said. Shall I knock?'

'I guess so,' I tell him. I can sense his nervousness
now — and I feel butterflies too. Will Charlie be here?
And, if he is, will he be pleased to see us?

14

The door opens and there's a shape in the doorway. A smoky, sweaty smell gusts out from inside. The voice that speaks is male, but sounds childlike. 'Hello. What do you want?'

'We're looking for Charlie,' says Kyle. 'Someone told us he might be here.'

'He's not,' the voice says firmly.

'But was he here?' I ask. 'Is he coming back?'

'He's gone. Last week. I don't think he's coming back. I like your dog.'

'Thanks,' I say.

Then I hear a voice from further inside, deeper, but still young. 'Hey, Reuben – who's at the door? We told you not to open the door to strangers.'

'They're not strange – they're nice,' Reuben calls back. 'It's a boy and a girl and a dog. He's a blind dog. They're looking for Charlie.'

'Well they ain't gonna find him here. Shut the door.'

'Wait!' I call. 'Do you have any idea where he is?'

'Zak!' Reuben calls. 'D'you know where Charlie is? Zak will tell you,' he says to us. 'He's nice, Zak. He's my brother. It's my house, but I live here with my brothers. Zak's kind and Jez buys me Heroes sometimes. They're chocolates. They're my favourites. Charlie doesn't like Heroes. He liked mints – lots of mints.' Reuben whispers this last bit conspiratorially, as if it's a big secret.

'Reubs, Jez told you to shut the door!' says a guy I guess is Zak. His voice isn't harsh – he actually sounds quite posh. 'Go back to your room, OK?'

'OK, bro,' says Reuben. 'I wish I could stroke your dog. It's sad he can't see.'

'It's me that can't see,' I explain. 'Samson can see – he guides me.'

'Oh. That's a nice name, Samson. I wish I had a dog.'

'Reuben! That's enough. I'll talk to them,' says Zak. 'Go on, off you go.'

'OK. Bye!' says Reuben.

'What's going on out there?' This is the first voice, presumably Jez, coming from inside the house – also male, but more authoritative.

Coming, Jez,' says Zak. 'You'd better go,' he tells us.

I'm not at all sure what's going on here, but I don't want him to close the door on us. Reuben says Charlie was here last week. This is the closest we've got.

'Is there any chance I could get some water for Samson?' I ask. 'Could you fill his bottle for me? It's so hot out and we've come a long way.'

I hear Zak tut.

'I'll get water for the dog!' I hear Reuben calling.

'I'll do it,' says Zak. 'Wait here.'

I was hoping we'd be able to go inside, but that's clearly not going to happen. Samson shuffles impatiently against my legs, clearly also wondering why we're standing here. I hear a phone ring. Then I hear swearing from inside – Jez. I hope I haven't got Zak into trouble.

'You'd better get that quick!' calls Jez. The phone stops ringing.

'Reuben?' I hear Kyle call softly. 'Are you there?'

'I would've got the water,' Reuben says, his voice coming nearer. 'Your dog's panting. He's thirsty, isn't he?'

'Yes,' I say.

'So, Charlie was here last week?' Kyle probes.

'I told you that already,' says Reuben. 'I have to go now.'

It's quiet.

'Has he gone?' I ask Kyle.

'Yes,' says Kyle.

'Water for the dog.' This isn't Zak, so I think it must be Jez.

'Thank you so much,' I say, holding out my hand until I feel the bottle pressed into it. 'Please, is there anything you can tell us about Charlie? Where he might be?'

'No. And if you want my advice, I'd stay right out of it. Keep away.'

'Why?' I ask. 'What's going on?'

'Jez, your phone's going off now!' Zak calls. 'I think it's Marty!'

'I gotta go,' says Jez. 'And you'd better too.'

I wait for the door to click, feeling instantly downhearted, but I don't hear it shut.

'You Charlie's family?' It's Zak's voice, speaking quietly. He must want to tell us something. 'It's nice you're looking for him. No one's going to come

107

looking for me.' He sounds sad.

'We're just mates,' Kyle explains. 'We don't want to bother you. It's just – if you know where he is . . .'

'I don't. But if you're going looking for him,' Zak says, his voice lowering to a whisper, 'you'd better have this. You might need it.'

I can't tell what Zak's giving Kyle, but I hear Kyle gasp and I catch a glint of something in his hand.

'What is it?' I ask at the same time as Kyle says, 'No, no!'

'Take it,' says Zak. 'You don't have to use it. Now put it away, quick.'

'W . . . why?' Kyle stutters.

'Just take care of yourselves,' says Zak. The door clicks shut.

'What did he give you?' I demand. 'What was it, Kyle?'

'I didn't take it. I've dropped it in the grass,' says Kyle.

'Was it money?' I ask.

'No. Come on. Let's get away from here.'

15

'Forward, Samson,' I instruct. 'Hup, hup.' Samson sets off happily, following Kyle.

'What was it?' I ask Kyle again when we're further away from the house.

'A knife,' he whispers.

'A *knife*?' I gasp. 'What? Why?'

Kyle sounds grim. 'Charlie must be mixed up in something bad.'

'I'm glad you didn't take it,' I tell Kyle. 'It was a weird set-up in that house, don't you think?'

'That Reuben – I think he's got learning difficulties,' says Kyle. 'He looked about twenty, but talked like an eight-year-old.'

'Reuben said they were his brothers,' I comment, 'but they all had different accents.'

'I think he meant "brothers" as in "mates".' They didn't exactly look like brothers. Different races and all that,' says Kyle.

'Maybe it's a foster home or care home?' I suggest. 'Maybe they're foster brothers? Reuben said they're kind to him.'

'Those boys weren't any older than us,' Kyle agrees. 'But if it's a home, where were the staff or foster parents?'

'Jez seemed to be in charge,' I comment. 'Though he moved fast when Zak said Marty was on the phone.'

'True,' says Kyle.

'So, we know Charlie was there, but we don't know why and we're no nearer to finding him,' I point out.

'What shall we do now?' Kyle asks, sighing.

At that moment my phone beeps with a text. I play it. **'How's your day going? What's Harwell House like? Dad.'**

'You don't want to go to Harwell House, do you?' I ask.

He laughs. 'So that you're not lying to your folks?'

'I do want to go anyway, but I'll understand if you want to get home.'

'No, let's go,' he says. 'But we might have to ask directions at that shop. We're coming up to it now.'

'You ask while I pour some water into Samson's bowl,' I suggest.

Harwell House turns out to be one of the most beautiful places I've ever been. It isn't just the incredible floral displays and the close-up pictures I manage to take of flowers I've never seen before, but the amazing multitude of scents and the birdsong and crickets chirping in the long grass too.

Kyle points out a butterfly on a flower and it actually stays still long enough for me to close in on it with my macro lens and catch it on camera. More than that, I actually see it – I think it's the first butterfly I've ever seen properly. It is patterned red and brown and stays put until Samson gets interested and gives it a sniff.

'Wouldn't it be amazing to live in a house like this and have all these grounds as your back garden?' I comment to Kyle.

'The house looks magnificent,' says Kyle. 'Shame it isn't open to the public. There's a photo on this info board of Lord and Lady Harwell.'

'Does Lord Harwell look like Charlie?' I ask.

Kyle laughs. 'You don't really think that could be

possible, do you – that he's Charlie's dad?'

'I know it's unlikely, but it would be a good reason for him to come to Harwell Heath,' I say. I step closer to the blurred rectangle that must be the board and move my face close enough to peer at it.

'He doesn't look much like him,' says Kyle.

'You're right,' I agree. 'Though I don't look much like my dad either.'

'This isn't a fairy tale,' Kyle says. 'Unless you want to ring the bell and ask him, I think you'd better forget the idea.'

'I wish it was true though,' I say. 'It would be a happy ending.'

I message Dad and attach a couple of photos. '**I'm having a lovely time.**'

'**Great!**' he answers instantly.

And I do have a lovely time. Kyle is quite happy to stand around, find interesting flowers and hold my bag while I take photos. Even Madz wouldn't be this patient.

'This isn't the sort of place I usually go to,' he tells me.

I'm photographing an incredible blue anemone when he suddenly says, 'Don't move, Libby!'

I freeze, wondering what's going on.

'You were about to tread on this,' Kyle says. 'Get your camera ready, quick!'

I put it to my eye and zoom in on the creature on his hand – a type of green beetle.

'Wow!' I click, click and click again. 'Can you put in on a leaf? I know it might not stay, but the picture will look more natural.'

He puts it carefully on a leaf in front of the blue flower. The result is magical.

'He's some kind of shield bug, I think,' says Kyle. 'That is such a good photo. You could enter Wildlife Photographer of the Year!'

'And you saved his life too,' I tell Kyle. 'You should get a medal.'

'I don't like to see insects squashed,' he tells me. 'Some of my monsters are inspired by insects.'

We stop at the café and I give Samson some more water in his folding water bowl, while Kyle and I have tuna sandwiches and a lemonade with ice. And then it's time to catch the train home.

On the train he asks to see my photos and I let him flick through on my camera.

'These are really good,' he says. 'I mean it, Libby.

You've got an eye . . .' He stops. 'Sorry, that's the wrong phrase.'

'Don't worry,' I say. 'I know what you mean. I think I do see things differently. I'm not distracted by everything all around because I can only focus on the details in front of my eyes.'

'That's probably it,' says Kyle. 'When I paint, I kind of close off what's around me and focus on the pictures in my mind.'

'Your mind is amazing, thinking up all that stuff,' I tell him.

'Thinking it is easy. The hard part is getting it down on paper.'

'Don't you love the feel of the paint, the way it slides off the brush to mark the paper?' I sigh.

'I've never thought about it, but yes, I do,' he says. 'It's our stop next. I know we didn't find Charlie, but I enjoyed today. I enjoyed being out with you.'

'Me too,' I say. I can feel my face hotting up and I am both happy and annoyed with myself.

Back at home I get down to my science homework. I have maths too, so I focus hard and get quite a lot done.

'Samson not with you?' Mum asks, when I come into the kitchen for dinner later. 'That's not like him.'

'We did a lot of walking today,' I tell Mum. 'He must be worn out.'

But when I go back upstairs after we've eaten, I sense instantly that something's wrong. Samson is lying in a strange position and there's a smell – like vomit. When I touch his head, he doesn't move it. My hand touches something sticky around his mouth.

'Samson! Samson! What's up, boy?'

He makes a slight huffing noise in response, but doesn't move.

Mum!' I yell. 'Get up here. It's Samson!'

'Oh gosh,' says Mum, coming in. 'He's been sick. What's he been eating?'

'Only his usual dog food,' I say. Then I think about the house – the water that Jez got for Samson. Jez didn't like us being there at all. And the other boy – Zak – tried to give Kyle a knife. Could Jez have put something in the water, drugs or something like that?

Has he poisoned Samson?

16

Mum calls the vet. I coax Samson to stand, but I can sense how wobbly and dazed he is. I wonder if he'll be able to manage the stairs, but I encourage him and he makes it down. He stands shakily by the door, as if waiting for his harness.

'Oh Samson,' I say gently, stroking his back. 'It's OK, you don't have to guide me. You're not well.' His tail flaps weakly.

'Mum, he will be OK, won't he?' I say, as she helps Samson into the car. I get in the back next to him. 'I couldn't bear it if anything happened to him. Mum?'

I don't like the long pause before Mum answers.

'Mum?' I say again.

'He will probably be OK, love,' says Mum. 'But I don't want to give false reassurance. It's unlikely, but possible that this is something serious. I don't know much about dogs, but I've never seen Samson

116

look like this.'

I feel panicky. 'But the vet will be able to do something. They have to.'

'Let's hope so,' says Mum.

Samson makes a strange gurgling noise. My stomach contracts. 'Mum!' I cry in dismay.

'Nearly there,' says Mum.

I can do nothing but sit tight and stroke Samson's warm back gently. At least he's still breathing. I sit beside him, my hand on his side, feeling his heart beating fast.

'It's OK, Samson,' I tell him. 'You'll be OK.'

I hope it's true. I couldn't bear anything to happen to Samson. He's not just my eyes – he's my friend, my companion. He understands me. I never imagined I could have such a close bond with an animal, a dog. I've never had a pet before. I looked after Mum's friend's dog for a couple of weeks while she was away before I applied for a guide dog, to show I was capable of looking after an animal. That dog was small and I did keep falling over her, but I enjoyed having her.

Samson is different though. He's amazing. He's so special. If I took him into danger . . . if he dies because we went to that place, I'll never forgive myself. Never. And what can I say to the vet? I can't say in front of Mum that Samson might have been drugged. I can't give away the fact that I was actually with Kyle and not Madz, and that we were looking for a boy from school, who's probably in trouble and might be running for his life.

I'm relieved that we don't have to wait long, though also a little afraid that this is because it is something serious. We are led into a room with a strong antiseptic smell that reminds me of hospitals. There's a big window so at least the room is bright.

'Hello, I'm Marie Caldwell, the senior vet here. So, Libby, this is your guide dog? What happened?'

I describe how I found him upstairs – and also mention that we'd been out for the day and that maybe he ate something he shouldn't have without me knowing.

'Let's have a look at him then,' says Marie. Her voice is kind and calm. 'I'll give him a thorough examination and hopefully we can find out what's wrong.'

'Libby,' says Mum. 'You can sit down in this chair if you like.' I hear a chair scrape as she pulls it across the floor. 'I'll put it here so you'll still be right beside him.'

She touches my hand and guides me to the chair. I sit and stroke Samson. I want to bury my head in his fur, but I don't want to get in the way.

I can sense the vet moving around Samson.

'What are you doing with him?' I ask her.

'I'm taking his temperature,' Marie tells me. 'It's a little high.'

Samson retches. 'Has he thrown up again?' I cry.

'It's just liquid,' says Mum.

'Don't worry – we're used to this kind of thing. I have an assistant here, James. He'll clear it up, won't you James?'

'Yep,' says a friendly voice.

'Could he have eaten something with rat poison in it?' Mum asks. 'I've heard of that happening.'

Ordinarily I'd butt in, pointing out that Samson isn't one to scavenge outside. He's been carefully trained not to do this. He may have wolfed down Joe's pancake – and he did once take a bite from a sandwich a girl was holding right next to him on a train – but that is rare and I think he thought the food was being given to him. I don't say this though. I want to hear what the vet thinks. If it's poison, then I'm sure I know who did it.

'It's possible,' says Marie. 'But it could just be an infection or virus. We'll run some blood tests and hope that will give us the answer. I'd quite like to keep him here overnight so we can keep an eye on him.'

'Do you have to?' I say.

'Libby,' says Mum. 'You want him to get better, don't you? He has the best chance here, with vets on hand if needed.'

I press my face into his fur. I don't care what anyone thinks. I am loath to be parted from Samson. We haven't had a night apart since I got him. I don't want to say it, but I'm scared he will die in the night and I might never see him again.

'I know it's hard for you,' says Marie. 'It's hard enough with a pet, but when you rely on him . . .'

'I love him so much,' I tell her.

'We'll do our best for him,' says Marie, softly.

'See you tomorrow, Samson,' I tell him. I touch his head, but he doesn't even move.

17

Mum guides me back to the car and I feel the tears streaming down my face.

'Oh, Libby. I'm sure he'll be fine,' Mum says. 'Take this tissue. Dry your eyes.'

I know she's trying to be supportive, but I kind of wish Dad was here. He'd be giving me a hug and telling me to 'just let it all out'.

Joe opens the door to us, asking anxiously, 'Where's Samson?'

'Oh Joe. They're keeping him in!' I tell him.

'Just to keep an eye on him while they get the test results,' Mum adds.

'Phew!' says Joe. 'I thought for a moment . . .'

I'm touched that Joe cares so much. 'Joe,' I say.

'He's gone back upstairs,' Mum tells me. 'At least he came to the door. That's more activity than I've seen from him in a while. Now, Libby – here's your cane. You'll need it if you're going anywhere.'

'I'm not,' I say firmly. 'I'm not going anywhere without Samson.'

'Love,' says Mum, 'you may have to. Even if he comes home tomorrow, he may need to rest for a few days.'

I go upstairs and lie miserably on my bed. I text Kyle. **'Samson's ill. I think he might have been poisoned. The water they gave me at the house???'**

He phones immediately and I am so grateful. I find myself crying, and instead of telling me to stop and not to worry he is immediately sympathetic. 'That's awful! I know they were keen to get rid of us, but to do that – to poison the water . . .'

'I don't know if they did,' I say quickly, between sobs. 'But if it was them, they must have wanted to warn us off, to make sure we kept away.'

'I was shocked enough when that boy tried to give me that knife,' says Kyle, 'but this is unbelievable. Poisoning a guide dog? If I wasn't scared that we'd get Charlie into more danger, I'd say let's call the police straight away.'

'What's going on?' I ask Kyle. 'What has Charlie got himself into?'

'I didn't like to say,' says Kyle, 'but that boy

Zak looked like he was spaced out on something. His eyes seemed weird, a bit like those homeless druggies near the station.'

'Maybe that's what they put in Samson's water!' I exclaim. I wonder if I should tell the vet, but that would mean admitting a whole bunch of stuff to Mum and Dad.

'I'm scared,' I tell Kyle. 'I wanted to find Charlie and help him, but this is too much.'

'You're right,' says Kyle. 'It's so messed up. I'm sorry about Samson. I hope he's OK.'

'So do I,' I tell him, still sobbing. 'So do I.'

I wake up very early on Monday and my first thought is Samson. I want to call the vet straight away, but Mum says they won't be open yet. I get dressed for school, but refuse breakfast and pace up and down between the hallway and the kitchen, waiting for the vet to open.

Dad comes down and says I should find something else to do. I go upstairs. I don't feel like doing anything, but I realise that I haven't had a proper look at all the photos I took at the botanical gardens at Harwell House. I zoom as large as I can and, with my eye close to the screen, enjoy the patterns and shapes, selecting those I think I might like to paint and those I'd just like to print out. I'm particularly pleased with the shield bug and the butterfly. My stomach rumbles and I remember my lack of breakfast.

I'm on my way back downstairs when I hear Mum's voice from the kitchen. 'Libby! You can call the vet now.'

Thoughts of breakfast vanish as I reach in my pocket for my phone.

'Samson?' says the vet's receptionist, 'Yes, he's perked up a lot this morning. He hasn't been sick again. We're still unclear about the cause.'

'Oh!' I'm relieved that's he's OK, but still worried about whether it was something in the water. 'Can we come and fetch him?'

'Maybe around four?' she suggests. 'Let us just keep an eye on him for a few more hours. And Libby, he'll need rest for a couple of days.'

My heart sinks. I'll have to manage with the cane. It's not that I can't. It's just that it's so much easier with Samson.

'How is he?' Dad asks. I tell him and I'm happy when Dad says he can leave work and take me to fetch him at four. 'Take care today,' says Dad. 'It's while since you've used that cane. Don't forget it isn't a dog.'

I jiggle my cane and woof at Dad, laughing. 'I do know that, Dad!'

I don't want to go to school though – I can't bear to go without Samson. And it's so long since I used my cane, I feel nervous about it. I admit this to Dad.

'I'd take you if I could, but I need to leave now,' says Dad. 'Maybe Madz would come early and walk with you?'

Madz is shocked to hear Samson is sick and says her mum can drop her at mine and we can walk from here.

'Thanks, Madz,' I say.

'I can guide you if you don't want to take your cane?' she says when she arrives at our house.

I take it though, explaining that even though I know she can guide me fine, the cane is a useful indicator to other people that I can't see. It helps them give me more space, as well as helping me find my own footing and recognise the kerb and any steps. I'd rather not be totally dependent on her.

*

Madz walks home with me at the end of the day too, babbling non-stop about Ollie, about how brilliant he is and all the things he does.

'He sounds too good to be true,' I can't help saying.

'Well, he's so perfect he makes me feel a bit useless sometimes,' she admits. 'Like when I went to the wrong cinema. And the other day I was rushing to get off a bus and my dress got caught and ended up with a black streak from the doors. But there he was, waiting, exactly on time and looking pristine. I almost wish he made a mess of things sometimes, just to make me feel better. How about Kyle? You seem to be with him every time I see you.'

'He's a good friend. I enjoy spending time with him,' I tell her.

'Just friends?' she teases.

'Yes,' I say firmly. I bat her with my cane, which is strictly against the rules.

Dad pulls up just as we reach my house and starts chatting to Madz. 'You enjoy yourself yesterday?' he asks her.

I feel instant panic.

'Yes – I had a good day,' Madz tells him. 'The

weather was lovely, wasn't it?'

'Come on, Dad – I want to get to Samson as quickly as possible,' I say before Madz gives away the fact that she wasn't with me at Harwell House. 'Thanks, Madz.'

'See you tomorrow!' says Madz.

Samson is so pleased to see me when we pick him up. He walks round and round me, pushing against me, and I tell him to stop as I know he's still weak. When we get home, I curl up with him close so I can feel his heart beating and I don't move for an hour.

18

'Where's your dog?'

I'm in the corridor at school, using my cane. Samson was desperate to come to school with me this morning. He couldn't understand why I was leaving him at home, but the vet said he had to rest, and I can tell he's still not quite himself. When I let him out in the garden, he usually runs around for at least ten minutes, but he was back at the door in less than two. He's been sleeping for long periods and I keep panicking and having to check him to make sure he's still breathing. I didn't want to leave him either, but I had to go to school.

'Libby! Where's Samson?'

I'm getting annoyed as I thought I'd told everyone yesterday. But I recognise this voice, and pull back against the wall, away from the crowds.

'Tia? Is that you?' I ask.

'Yeah.' She comes up close.

'Samson's ill,' I explain.

'Oh – I hope he's better soon,' she says. 'You still looking for my brother?'

'Sort of,' I tell her. 'But we've run out of ideas.'

'You know my dad's gone off now?' says Tia.

'Oh – I'm sorry,' I say in surprise. 'What happened?'

'After you came round, Mum and Dad had a row. She's angry that he never told her what he said to Charlie. Dad stormed out. He's gone to stay with Auntie Gwen. Mum thinks he'll come back when he's cooled off.'

'He should have told her,' I agree, relieved that Tia isn't blaming me and Kyle for all this.

'I reckon Charlie could be looking for his real dad,' says Tia. 'I would, if I was him.'

'We think so too. Do you think your mum might tell us anything else about him – Charlie's birth dad?' I ask. 'Anything that might help us find him?'

'After Dad went, Mum looked through her old papers,' says Tia. 'It must have stirred stuff up for her, I guess, and she wanted to see what she had. She said she's sure the papers weren't in the order she'd left them in the box. And Charlie's birth certificate was missing. She's pretty sure it was in there. It had his real dad's name on it.'

'You think Charlie took it?' I say. 'Then you're right – it makes sense that he really has gone looking for his dad.'

'Yeah,' says Tia. 'Charlie got himself in a mess – he can't blame anyone else for that, but I do feel a tiny bit sorry for him about his dad. That must've been such a shock. Hey, we'd better get to class. The bell's about to ring.'

I keep thinking about Charlie, wondering what chance he'd have of finding his real dad, with only his name.

I have lunch with Kyle and tell him what Tia said.

'Perhaps we could go to Charlie's house,' I suggest, 'and ask his mum to have another look in her box of papers. Maybe Charlie found something else – an old address for his dad, even. Maybe he could still be living there . . .'

'We can ask her, I guess,' says Kyle. 'She can only say no.'

'We can ask Tia to ask her for us,' I say.

So after school we find ourselves walking back with Tia.

'You're really that keen on finding him?' his mum says, when we reach the house. She sounds like she finds this hard to believe. 'I hope he realises what good friends he has. Maybe I was too hard on him, but I gave him enough chances. I tried to get help for him too. He threw it all back in my face.'

'We just want to know he's OK,' I say, feeling guilty. I certainly wouldn't call Charlie a friend of mine, and I don't think Kyle would either.

I hear a clunk as she puts a box down on the kitchen table. 'I don't think there's anything useful here,' says Charlie's mum. 'There's a couple of letters and postcards, but they just say "Johnny" on them. No address.'

I can hear her flicking through papers.

'Oh – here – look! I've got a photo,' she says. 'I didn't see this before! There's no name on it so Charlie wouldn't have known – and anyway, it was stuck between these two cards. He can't have seen it when he looked in here. This is Johnny.'

'Let's see,' says Tia.

'I didn't even know I'd kept this!' says her mum. 'I'd forgotten how good-looking he was.'

'Can I see?' I ask.

'What?' She sounds surprised.

'If I hold things close to my eyes, I can see them,' I explain.

She hands me the picture and I hold it close, but the figure is small and there isn't much contrast so I can't really see.

'Do you mind if I take a picture of it with my phone?' I ask. 'Then I can blow it up big.' I don't know why, but I want to see it, this picture of the man who is really Charlie's dad.

'If you want,' says his mum.

I click my phone and then zoom in. Now I can make out the face of a man in his twenties with light hair. He's sitting at a table – I think there's food in front of him. And he's smiling.

Kyle's arm brushes against me as he leans in to have a look too. I feel him jolt.

'You all right?' I ask.

'Libby,' he says. 'I've just remembered I've got to get home – my uncle's coming over. We'll have to go.' He turns away from me. 'Thanks for showing us this.'

Once we're outside, I expect Kyle to walk away fast, but he doesn't.

'I thought you were in a rush,' I remind him.

'It was an excuse,' he explains. 'I had a shock. A big shock. I had to get out of there.'

'The photo?' I ask. 'Do you mean you recognised him – Charlie's real dad?'

'I know this is gonna be hard to believe,' he says, walking even slower. 'But I promise you. It's him. His face is imprinted on my brain.'

I've no idea what he's getting at, but there's a weird tone to Kyle's voice and I feel my heart fluttering. I have a sudden thought. 'He's not that guy, is he – the Lord of Harwell House?'

'What?' Kyle sounds bewildered. 'No, of course not.'

I feel myself blushing. 'Who then?' I demand. 'Whose face?'

'There's a bench here – let's sit a minute. I can't catch my breath.'

He guides me to the bench and I sit, balancing my cane between my knees. 'You'd better get on and explain before I crack up,' I tell him.

I hear Kyle take a deep breath. 'You remember I told you how Charlie saved my life?'

'When you got abducted in a car?' I say.

'Yes,' says Kyle. 'Well, the man in the photo is the man who was driving that car. I'm certain. It's the same man.'

19

'What?' I say. 'How? What does this mean?'

'What if Charlie finds him?' says Kyle, his voice wavering. 'His dad – a man like that. He tried to *abduct* us. He's bad news.'

This doesn't quite make sense to me. And as I play around with Kyle's words in my head, I realise why.

'Hang on,' I say. 'Don't you think it's a bit of a coincidence that this man gets two kids into his car and one of them happens to be his son?'

'What?' says Kyle.

'Do you think he might have known?' I go on. 'That Charlie was his son? He might have just wanted to see him – to spend time with him. And it all went wrong . . .'

'What?' says Kyle. 'I never thought –' He pauses for a moment, then says, 'You could be right . . .' And his voice tails off.

'His mum said he wanted to make a go of it – to

135

be a family,' I remind Kyle. 'But when she said no, he just left. Maybe later he changed his mind, and was curious about his son.'

'So he's not a child abductor?' Kyle says quietly. 'He didn't mean us any harm?'

I can hear that he's struggling to take this in.

'I could be wrong,' I tell him, touching his knee gently, 'but it makes sense. It was a stupid thing he did, to offer you both a lift. But if he'd been watching Charlie – if he could see how wet you were getting in the rain – it might've just been an impulse, and once he had you in the car, he didn't want to just drop you off quickly. He wanted a bit of time with Charlie. I can imagine it like that. And after you ran off, he must've been so scared you'd go to the police. And he couldn't try to make contact with Charlie again after that, could he?'

'I've always felt so lucky to have escaped,' says Kyle, his voice sounding like a faded impression of itself. 'The things I've imagined that he'd have done to us if Charlie hadn't got us out. I used to wake up from nightmares about it. It made me realise how scary the world can be – how in one moment you can go from being a normal kid, running home in the

136

rain, to being the victim of a terrible crime . . .'

'Stop, Kyle!' I beg him, squeezing his arm.

'Sorry,' he says. And I see the shape of his arm going up towards his eyes.

I stroke his arm. I think he's crying, but it's not until he sniffs that I know for sure. 'Are you OK?' I ask gently. 'Do you need a tissue? I've got one in my bag.'

'It doesn't make sense,' he says, sniffing again. 'Why am I upset to find out the guy I thought was some terrifying child abuser, was probably just Charlie's real dad wanting time with his son?' He sniffs again.

'Here.' I fiddle with the zip of my bag and pull out a tissue. He takes it and blows his nose noisily.

'Sorry,' he says again. 'You must think I'm pathetic.'

'Of course not!' I exclaim in horror. 'Why would I? There was no possible way you could have known.'

'If it wasn't for you, I don't think I'd have even worked it out now,' says Kyle. 'But the more I think about it, the more I'm sure you're right.' He sniffs again. 'If Charlie does find his dad, I wonder how his dad will react.'

'I hope he'll be pleased to see him – and help him. If someone still wants to kill Charlie, he needs help.'

'But his dad could have a new partner and more children by now,' Kyle points out. 'He might not want to know. Anyway, how could Charlie find him with just the name?'

'So it's still up to us to help him,' I say. 'Perhaps you could look for images of Johnny Hunter online and see if you can recognise him?'

'I guess that's worth a go,' says Kyle. 'Can you forward me that photo?'

I scroll and wait to hear 'photos' and select the last one I took, forwarding it to Kyle's phone.

'Thanks,' he says.

'Are you OK?' I ask.

'Yeah. But I still feel kind of weird. Everything's shifted off-balance. What I believed isn't true.'

'Maybe the nightmares will stop,' I suggest.

'I hope so,' says Kyle. 'I'm just thinking – Charlie didn't really save my life.'

'No, but he thought he did,' I remind him. 'He pulled you out of that car when you both thought you were being abducted. He was brave.'

'That's true,' says Kyle.

'I'm thinking,' I tell him, 'the only other lead we have is that house in Harwell Heath. Charlie was there. I'm sure one of them must know more. Maybe we should have pressed harder for information.'

'There was something scary about that place,' Kyle reminds me. 'What about the poison in Samson's water? And that boy Zak tried to give me a knife. I'm not mad about going back there.'

'We still don't know for sure if Samson was poisoned,' I say. 'I'm not crazy about going there again either. I just think maybe we should try.'

My phone buzzes. I pull it out, scroll and listen to the message. It's a text from Dad. '**Where are you and who are you with?**'

'**I'm on my way home,**' I reply.

His question makes me nervous. I gave him the impression that I was going to Madz's place to do homework together, though I didn't directly mention Madz. So why is asking now? Has something happened?

'I just need to call my dad,' I tell Kyle.

I phone him and he picks up instantly.

'What's up, Dad?' I ask.

'I thought you were with Madz, at her house,' he says.

'I was.' It's a lie – and I regret it the moment it slips from my lips.

'No, you weren't,' he says sternly.

'I was – but I'm not with her now,' I say.

'I know you're not because she's here!' says Dad. 'She says she hasn't seen you all day and she thinks you might be out with a boy. Is that true?'

I am instantly mad at Madz. Why did she have to tell Dad that? And why has she just turned up at mine?

'Oh, Dad, I'm fine,' I tell him. 'You don't need to worry. I *was* out with a boy, but I'm not going out with him or anything. We're just friends.'

'I think you should come home right now,' says Dad.

Then he's gone.

20

'You didn't tell your folks about me?' Kyle asks. He sounds surprised.

'Only because I knew they'd make a fuss. They worry about me, especially Dad,' I explain.

My phone rings again. This time it's Madz.

'I'm sorry, Libs. I came round to see you. I was so upset – Ollie dumped me! I didn't know you'd lied to your dad and he was so frantic about where you were and who you were with, that I told him you were probably with Kyle. I wish you'd told me I was meant to be covering for you.'

'Madz – I'm in a right mess, thanks to you!' Maybe I shouldn't have said this, but I'm angry. I end the call.

'Come on. I'll walk you home,' says Kyle. 'And if it helps, I can come in and explain. Maybe if your dad meets me he will realise I'm OK?'

'That's kind, but I think I should talk to him first,'

I say. 'Once he's calmed down.'

'Will you be OK?' Kyle asks.

He sounds so caring, I am touched.

'My dad's a softy really. He was just worried.'

But I can feel the atmosphere at home as I walk through the door. It's like the air is crackling. Dad is literally fuming. I've never known him as angry as this.

'Is Madz still here?' I ask him.

'No, she's long gone,' he says gruffly. 'Sit down, Libby. We need to have a proper talk about this.'

I sit on the edge of the sofa. Samson hasn't come down and I'm suddenly worried. I long for his warmth, the comfort of him at my feet right now.

'Is Samson OK?' I ask.

'Yes, he's sleeping in your room,' says Dad.

I decide to try to pre-empt his lecture by getting in first. 'I'm sorry, Dad – I really am. I should have told you about Kyle.'

'Too right, you should.' This is Dad's 'teacher' voice which I so rarely hear at home. When he does use it, it's normally directed at Joe, not me.

'I trusted you,' Dad goes on. 'You wanted more

independence and your mother convinced me that we should encourage you.'

'I know,' I say. 'And I didn't plan for any of this to happen. I –'

'I have to say, I am very disappointed,' Dad cuts in. 'Do you have any idea of the stress and worry you gave me? I thought you were safe at Madz's house and suddenly I learn you could be anywhere, with anyone! And you'd lied, which implied you were up to something you didn't want me to know about. That was even more of a worry.'

'Madz got a boyfriend, Ollie,' I tell Dad, 'so I wasn't seeing so much of her. Then Kyle started being friendly and we took Samson to the park together. We hung out together. He's nice – really nice. We're not dating, Dad, but I was worried how you'd react if I wanted to go out with a boy.' This isn't the truth, I know, but I can't tell Dad the real reason.

'It's not just that he's a boy,' says Dad. 'More that he's someone we don't know at all. We don't know anything about him. We know Madz so well. We know we can rely on her to be there for you. When I mentioned Harwell House and your lovely photos,

Madz clearly knew nothing about any of that either. You went with this Kyle, didn't you?'

'Yes,' I admit. 'But I was fine, wasn't I? I feel safe with Kyle, or I wouldn't be hanging out with him. I'm not stupid, Dad.'

'I still don't get it,' says Dad. 'If Kyle's such a nice boy, why did you have to lie about him? I feel like you're hiding something.'

'It was wrong,' I admit. 'And I'm sorry.'

'I'm sorry too, Libby. You want to be treated like a normal teenager, so I'm going to ground you for a week. No going out after school or next weekend. Do you understand? And as I can't trust you, I'll have to make sure Gran is here every afternoon, like before.'

'Oh, Dad, that's not fair! And what about Gran? She has her own life now. When will she get to see Dominic? Please – just meet Kyle? I'm sure once you meet him you'll change your mind.'

'Kyle was happy to go out with you, knowing we didn't know where you were or who you were with?' says Dad. 'He sounds completely irresponsible too.'

'He didn't know!'

'Well, when you're no longer grounded, perhaps then I'll think about meeting him,' Dad says.

I go up to my room and hug Samson. He gets up and wags his tail, then pushes his nose against my face. I think he can tell I'm upset. I know I did the wrong thing. I feel so bad about it, but grounding for a week feels a bit extreme. I've never, ever been anywhere with anyone without telling my parents before all this. And I am fifteen! But I should have told them. I wish I'd told them.

Kyle texts. 'All OK?'

'Grounded for a week,' I tell him.

'Sorry.'

'It's my fault.'

'Still sorry,' he replies. 'Sad emoji,' my phone adds. 'Looked for images of Johnny Hunter,' he goes on, 'but haven't found anything. Thinking about going back to that Harwell Heath house.'

'You shouldn't go on your own,' I tell him. Then I feel foolish, as if I'm implying he'll be safer with me. 'Sorry,' I add, before he can respond. 'Didn't mean that. I'm not your bodyguard.'

'I'd rather go together, but if you're grounded . . .'

'It's a pain. Just be careful. Keep in touch.'

I groom Samson gently. He loves being brushed. He gives me a lick — I think he's trying to groom me back, or maybe he senses I'm feeling down. I think about Madz, feeling bad. Maybe I should call her now and be supportive, but I'm not in the mood. I still feel like I'm grounded because of her. I want to go with Kyle, not be stuck here feeling useless.

As I reach down to stroke Samson again, I'm thinking about Charlie's dad. I get out my phone and zoom in on the photo. Kyle said he couldn't find him online. I wish there was some way that I could. Then at least I'd feel like I was doing something.

Then I have a thought. I'm not sure it's possible, but I know who to ask.

I knock on Joe's door and go in. Joe has the curtains drawn and it's very dark. If I didn't know the position of his desk, I wouldn't know where he was. There's a strong animal scent.

'Joe, is it possible to scan a photo and then search for any other images of the same person online?'

'I know how to do that,' says Joe. 'Who are you looking for?'

'This guy,' I say, holding out the photo. 'Only this was taken at least fifteen years ago, so he might have changed a lot.'

'I can try for you, see what comes up,' he offers.

'Thanks, that'd be great. Can I put the light on in here?'

'Sure.' Joe takes my phone. 'I can press this here, and this app scans the face and looks for matches. You can do it with things too. If you take a photo of a castle you go past, you can scan it and it'll tell you the name.'

'Does anything come up for that photo?' I ask.

'Lots. But most of them don't look that much like him,' says Joe. 'Maybe it's easier with castles than with faces. Hang on – this might be him.' I hear the tap of the keyboard. 'Morgan Bridgeworth,' says Joe.

'No, that's not him,' I say.

'Wait, this is better. I'm sure this is the same guy. I'm following the link,' says Joe. 'It's a printing company in Birmingham. He's one of the managers. There's photos of the team. His name's Johnny Hunter.'

I gasp. 'Yes – that's him! I had the name already,

but it's such a common name we had no idea where to start. Thanks, Joe! You've helped so much. Let me have a look.'

I zoom in, enlarging the screen so I can see the face and name for myself. There's an email address.

'I'll write down that email address for you,' says Joe. He hands me a slip of paper.

I can hear Dad banging about in the kitchen, making supper. I wish he would appreciate how being friends with Kyle has helped with my independence skills – going out with different people, going to new places. Mum would understand that. Maybe I can convince her to talk Dad into reducing the grounding.

I text Kyle eagerly to tell him I've found Charlie's dad. He doesn't reply. Feeling impatient, I phone him but it goes to voicemail. I leave a message for him to call me. I have a slight sinking feeling. Why hasn't he responded? Did he go the house in Harwell Heath? Has something happened? I try to push these thoughts away. He's probably just busy. At least I'll see him tomorrow at school. I can tell him then.

But the next morning he still hasn't replied to my text. When I try to find him at school before form time, no one I ask has seen him. Maybe he's running late. My heart sinks further. If he went back to Harwell Heath last night and hasn't come back – then I have good reason to be worried.

21

'I'm sorry, Libby.'

I'm glad to hear Madz's voice. We walk to class
together.

'I'm sorry too,' I tell her. 'It's not your fault I got
into trouble. I should have told you what I was doing.'
I realise I've shown her no sympathy about Ollie yet,
and I feel a sudden guilt. 'Are you OK? What
happened with Ollie?' I ask.

Madz sighs. 'We were getting on so well, but then
suddenly he went cold. And when I asked what was
up, he said he was getting back together with Kayleigh.
You know, he was going out with her before me.'

'Oh no – that's awful,' I say.

'I think I was just there to fill time, or make
Kayleigh jealous,' Madz says bitterly. 'I feel so stupid.'

'You're not stupid,' I assure her. 'How were you
to know?'

'He's treated me badly, but I still miss him,' sniffs

Madz. 'How are things with Kyle?'

'We're not going out,' I remind her. 'He's just a friend.'

'But do you really like him? Or have you just been hanging out because of me and Ollie?' Madz asks.

'What, like copying you?' I ask, bristling a little.

'You know that's not what I mean! But I realise I did kind of abandon you. I shouldn't have done that, Libs.'

'It's fine,' I tell her. 'It's good that I learn not to rely on you too much. And Kyle's OK. I've grown to like him more and more.'

'So you do *like* him?' Madz teases.

'You don't give up, do you?' I laugh. Then I sigh. 'The thing is, I don't think he's in school today and I'm worried. I can't get hold of him.'

'Maybe he's ill,' Madz says.

'Maybe – but I think he'd have contacted me if he wasn't coming to school.'

I wonder if it's finally time to tell Madz about how we've been looking for Charlie – but somehow it doesn't feel right. That's between me and Kyle.

'I'm sure he'll turn up,' she says.

I hope she's right. Perhaps he's just stayed home

to look after his mum, like he said he sometimes does. But why hasn't he let me know? It doesn't stop me worrying though. And he doesn't appear all day.

When I get home, Gran is there and she's not very happy.

'Oh Libby,' she says. 'I'm so disappointed in you. I keep thinking it must be my fault for saying you should find yourself a nice boy.'

'It's nothing to do with you, Gran,' I tell her.

'I was supposed to be helping Dominic with some gardening today,' says Gran. 'He's got an allotment, but he's having trouble keeping on top of it. I was looking forward to it, especially as the weather's not so hot.'

'I'm sorry Gran. I didn't want to stop you from seeing him. I told Dad that. It really isn't necessary.'

'Well, I suppose I can help Dominic another time,' says Gran. 'I don't want him to overdo it – not after his heart attack.'

The afternoon drags. I'm worrying about Kyle and Gran's worrying about Dominic.

The next day, Kyle still isn't in school. Now I am seriously worried. But I don't know what to do. I don't even know where he lives. I call him again and leave another message.

The day after, Miss Peters asks, 'Does anyone know why Kyle isn't in school?'

So this means he hasn't called in sick. I wonder again if he went back to Harwell Heath alone, and if something happened to him while he was there. But surely his mum would have reported him missing if so? As I battle down the panic in my stomach, I wonder if I should tell Miss Peters everything – about the note, Charlie. But maybe that will make things worse. And what if it puts Kyle in danger?

Someone approaches me in the corridor at break.

'Libby, it's Jenny. I need to talk to you about the theatre trip tomorrow. Do you have time to come to my office now?'

I go with Jenny. I don't like to admit I'd forgotten all about the theatre trip and how Jenny said she would sort out any extra help I'd need. I've had so much else on my mind.

'So, I've just had a call from the theatre and they've offered you the opportunity to come early and have a touch tour of the set,' says Jenny. 'I know it's short notice, but you'll get so much more out of the play.'

'Thank you,' I say. 'It'd be great to do that.'

'It means going separately from the main group, and I know you said both your parents are working. Is there someone who can take you? Unfortunately, I can't do it as I have another student to support.'

'Could I go with Madz?' I ask. 'She's used to guiding me and I'll have Samson too.'

'Fine with me. But I'll have to check with Madz and her parents, and also with yours. You'll need to get there by one thirty. It's one train and then a five-minute walk,' Jenny continues. 'The rest of the group will arrive for the performance at three, and you'll be able to go back with everyone on the coach afterwards.'

I'm pleased when I hear that Madz and her parents are fine about her coming to the theatre early with me. And Mum is home, so I ask her rather than Dad. As this is a school thing, she agrees.

'Just be sensible – and no more lies,' she tells me.

I'm also relieved that Samson is back to his usual bouncy self and will be able to come too. I try to think about the theatre trip and not about Kyle, but he is still at the forefront of my mind. I just wish he'd call me.

On the way to the theatre the next day, I can't help talking about him.

'I suppose it's a bit odd, but I wouldn't worry too much,' says Madz. Then she starts talking about how she saw Ollie chatting up another girl, even though he's meant to be back with Kayleigh. 'I was an idiot, Libs. He sucked me in like a hoover.'

Once she's finished on Ollie, she gives me a running commentary, very quietly, about the people on the train. 'There's a woman who's got so many bags she looks like she's doing her Christmas shopping six months early. And there's another woman with the cutest puppy with its head sticking out of her handbag. You should see Samson's face! He's staring at it, shaking his head, like the puppy should be ashamed not to be standing on its own four feet. OMG, that man is actually wearing odd shoes. They don't match! Do you think it's deliberate, or he just didn't notice when he put them on?'

That's the thing I love about Madz – she makes me laugh. And, a bit like the tour of the set we're about to have, she helps me experience what's going on around me. I would miss so much otherwise.

It's not all fun though. I hear someone muttering, 'Poor dog. It shouldn't be allowed. Why do blind people think they have the right to make dogs work for them?'

I'm too stunned to say anything, but Madz jumps in. 'Why do stupid people think they have the right to keep dogs shut indoors all day while they're at work?'

'Yes,' I add, boosted by Madz's support. 'I love my dog, and Samson loves what he does for me.'

The woman doesn't respond.

'Well done,' says Madz to me. 'You'd never have spoken up like that a few months back.'

'I'm glad you're with me though,' I tell her. 'I wouldn't have dared otherwise.'

22

The touch tour at the theatre is amazing. We get to go on set and touch the props and the scenery while a woman describes it all to me. I even get to touch the costumes.

'I'm sorry this performance won't be audio-described,' the woman explains as she shows me where we'll be sitting. 'We have one audio-described performance next week.'

'What, like the cinema?' I say.

'It's not quite like the cinema,' says the woman. 'You do wear headphones, but it's live, not pre-recorded, so that the timing is right for the specific performance. Maybe mention it to school, so it's something they can think about next time. And if you're coming with your family, do make enquiries first.'

'I can audio-describe for you,' Madz suggests.

'I think you'd be great,' I tell her, 'but I'm not

sure the people sitting near us would appreciate it.'

'I'll do an audio-described performance for you on the coach home, then.'

I laugh. I'm sure that'll be something to look forward to.

I enjoy the show so much. The stage is a blur apart from the bright lights above, but there's a lot of dialogue and the voices are distinctive, making it easier. The touch tour beforehand made a big difference. I've been to couple of theatre shows before, including school productions, but never enjoyed one as much as this because I really could follow what was going on.

After the performance, we all pile on to the coach back to school, and Madz is as good as her word as she starts to audio-describe the play.

'The stage is set for breakfast. Marcia enters left wearing a pink dressing gown – you know, that fluffy one you touched?'

'Is this going to be an interactive audio-description then?' I say.

'As it's a completely personal service, I'd say yes,' says Madz. 'So feel free to ask me questions as we go along.'

Madz carries on, and I'm surprised when other people start chipping in.

'You forgot the bit with the grandad!' someone yells.

Then there are arguments about what certain people were wearing at certain points, and even whether they exited the set right or left. It is so lovely to spend time with Madz like this, and for things to feel normal after everything that's happened in the last few days.

The whole coach is laughing hysterically by the end.

'And I think that's it,' says Madz finally. 'And now I am taking a bow.'

'I haven't had such a laugh in ages,' I tell her as everyone claps. 'You really could get a job doing this.'

'Maybe I'll think about it,' she says, laughing too.

'I see you have permission to walk home,' says Miss Ahmed when the coach drops us off at school. 'Will you be OK?'

'I'm fine now with the walk to school and back on my own,' I say. 'And I have Samson.'

I say goodbye to Madz and walk towards home,

cutting down the path by the station, still thinking about the play. When Samson yanks me sideways into the bushes, I nearly stumble. This isn't like him. I wonder if today's been too much for him, and he's still not fully recovered from his illness.

'What's up, boy?'

I try to pull him back towards the path, but he doesn't want to move. He seems alert, ears pricked – not sick. I trust Samson. There must be a reason for this. He's keeping me safe. I stand still, listening for a clue, but I can't hear anything. No sudden breeze of a passing cyclist or child whizzing by on a scooter. Nothing.

Samson's head is now down as if he's sniffing something. Of course, dogs like to sniff things. If someone has dropped half a hot dog or a burger, any dog could be tempted, even a well-trained guide dog.

'Hey, Samson! What's up?' I ask again, softly touching his back.

Samson replies by sitting down. Maybe his tummy is hurting. Maybe he's cut a paw on some glass on the path. I crouch beside him, stroking his head.

'It's all right, boy,' I tell him. I feel his legs, lift each paw gently and examine it with my fingers. The pads feel normal and he doesn't wince at the touch. Instead he nuzzles against me and then pushes my hand towards the long grass with the wild flowers I often stop to photograph. Beyond this grassy area is a fence and then the railway line. Dad doesn't like me coming here. He says it's too quiet, but that's why I like it. There's no danger of traffic.

Right now, Samson's nose seems to be pointing towards a blue flower: a cornflower, waving in the breeze. It's as if he's found me a perfect flower to photograph. I lean down, pulling the stem gently close to my eyes. Each delicate purple petal has zig zag edges and the centre is darker purple. It looks as if it has been designed on paper, and then created intricately with hours and hours of hand crafting. I want to pull out my camera from my bag, but Samson nudges me. He seems upset. His body is tense, not relaxed. His nose is pointing down, into the grass. I push my hand forward and further down between the grasses, and that's when I touch it.

Something that feels a bit like – a finger.

I gasp. It can't be. It must be something else. Gingerly I slide my hand along. There are more finger-like things, soft like skin but cold and stiff.

I can feel the ridges of the knuckles. Then I feel the hand and the arm. Now I'm sure.

The hand is cold and stiff. The fingers don't bend.

I pull back. I'm as sure as I can be.

It's a body. A dead body in the grass.

23

I feel a sharp pang in my chest and suddenly understand what people mean when they say 'my heart skipped a beat'. I'm frozen to the spot, as if my heart has stopped – as if everything has stopped. Even time itself.

Maybe I should lean over and look properly, but I don't want to get that close. I know what's there. I don't have to see more to be certain. Could it be Charlie? Or Kyle?

I pull out my phone and call Madz. She won't be far away. We only parted a few minutes ago. I'm so relieved when she picks up.

'Can you come?' I say. 'I'm on the path from the station.'

'What's happened?'

'Just come – quickly, please!'

It feels like I'm waiting ages. It suddenly seems too quiet here, and I don't want to be alone. I try to tell myself I've made a mistake. Maybe it's a dummy – not a real person.

'Libby!'

I am so relieved to hear Madz's voice. I turn to face her, her blurry shape getting bigger as she comes nearer.

'Libby! What's going on?'

'There's something – someone . . . down there – in the long grass. Look . . .' I don't want to say the word.

Madz leans down and then cries out. 'Oh my gosh! Oh Libby! Oh my gosh!'

'It's a body, isn't it?' I whisper.

'Oh Libby! Oh my gosh!'

I can hear her breathing, fast and loud.

'Calm down,' I tell her. 'Don't have a panic attack. It's a body, isn't it?'

'Yes,' says Madz.

'Can you see . . . who it is?'

'Oh Libby,' she whispers, and I can hear her breath coming even faster. 'Oh Libby . . . He's face down – there's blood, Libby. A lot of blood.'

I raise my hand. 'Stop! I don't want an audio-description. I just want to know who . . . Is it Kyle?'

'No,' she tells me. 'This dead guy – he's shorter and his hair is darker.'

Relief surges through me but I feel wobbly. I know it can't be Charlie either, because he's blond.

'How did you . . . how did you find him there?' Madz asks.

'It wasn't me. It was Samson.'

I feel more than wobbly now – giddy, disorientated. There's a dead body in the grass – right here. But it's not Kyle or Charlie. I press my hand on Samson's back for support and am grateful for the warmth and softness of his fur. I stroke him gently.

'We should call the police,' I tell Madz, 'and probably an ambulance too.'

'Yes.'

I can hear Madz breathing and Samson huffing gently. I feel my legs buckling. Samson snorts.

'Madz,' I urge. 'Shall I call? Or will you do it?'

'I . . . I . . .' Madz is clearly in no state to do anything.

'I'll call,' I tell her, 'but I'll have to hand over to you to say what you can see.' I hold my phone to my mouth. 'Call nine-nine-nine,' I tell it. I put it to my ear and hear it ringing.

'Emergency, which service do you require?' says a woman's voice.

'Police,' I tell her, 'and ambulance, I guess. But the person – he's already dead.' I give my name and phone number and our location and hand over to Madz to describe the scene. She takes the phone, but she doesn't speak.

'Madz!' I prompt.

'I . . . I can't,' she says. 'I don't want to look at him again.'

I get a snatch of a voice speaking to her. The 999 woman can clearly hear what Madz is saying. 'OK,' Madz tell her, taking a deep breath. 'There's blood – a lot of blood. I think he's been stabbed.'

I swallow. I'm feeling shaky now. I text Kyle. **'Where are you? Please message me!'**

My relief that it isn't him is overwhelming. As we wait for the police, I need to distract myself. I remember the cornflower and get out my camera.

'You're not going to take photos of him?' Madz asks in horror.

'No – just that flower over there,' I tell her, pointing. 'It's just so I don't have to think about him – lying there . . .'

Click, click. The sound, the focus, is calming me.

Madz is not calm. Her breathing is too fast. Her vague shape suddenly disappears from view.

'Madz? Where've you gone?'

'H-here, I'm just s-s-s-sitting d-d-down,' she says between sobs. She reaches up, touches my knee. I sit down beside her and squeeze her hand. Samson burrows his head into my lap on the other side.

24

A policewoman finally arrives. It's probably only five minutes since we called, but it feels much longer.

'Was it you that called us?' she asks.

'Yes,' says Madz quietly. 'I'm Madz.'

'I'm Libby,' I say. 'I found him. Well, Samson did.'

'Ah,' says the policewoman. 'I'm DC Baron. Hello Libby. Well done, Samson. You're a good dog, aren't you?'

Samson shifts beside me.

So, where . . . ?' says DC Baron.

'Over there in the grass,' says Madz.

'I see,' says DC Baron. 'And have you moved him or touched him at all?'

'I touched him – just his finger and hand,' I tell her. 'I knew he was dead. We didn't touch him after that. Do you know who he is?'

'No,' says DC Baron. 'But I'm sure we'll soon

find out.'

More police are here now, dark shadowy shapes moving around. There are white shapes moving too – maybe forensics. I wonder if I should tell them about Charlie, and about Kyle, who I feel sure must count as missing too. He still hasn't replied to my text.

But that will mean I'll be questioned. The police will want to know why I haven't called them before. But there's no connection with this body. I don't have to say anything.

The police ask for our details and take a statement. Then they offer to take us home. We agree gratefully, even though it isn't far.

Samson's already up and I feel the slight strain on the harness as we set off towards the end of the alley where the police car is parked. I'm taking one step after another, but I feel as if I'm walking on cotton wool rather than the path.

Madz guides me into the back of the police car. Her arm is shaking.

'Do you want me to come back with you?' I ask her.

'No – it's OK,' says Madz. 'Mum's home. I'll be fine.'

*

When we reach my house, DC Baron rings the bell, but no one comes so I scrabble in my bag for my key. My hand is wobbly and she offers to open the door for me. Then I'm in.

'Libs! Is that you?' Dad calls from upstairs. 'How was the show? I thought you'd be back earlier. Was the traffic bad?'

'Can you come down, Dad?' I call. I feel for the bottom step of the staircase and sit down, unclipping Samson's harness. I'm suddenly exhausted. Tears start to slip down my face, and Samson noses me and tries to lick them away. I stroke his head and hug him.

'Oh Samson! I love you so much,' I tell him. 'And you did a good job. Otherwise he might still be lying there . . .' Samson flaps his tail against my legs.

The stairs vibrate as Dad comes down. 'Oh – hello,' he says, seeing the policewoman. 'What's wrong?'

'Your daughter's had rather a shock,' says DC Baron. 'She found a body.'

'A body! What on earth . . . ?'

'I'll leave your daughter to explain,' DC Baron says. 'I just wanted to make sure she was home safely.'

'Thank you,' says Dad, showing her out.

'What's going on, Libby?' he asks me as soon as she's gone. 'I presume you did actually go to the theatre with Madz, and weren't off with that boy?'

'Of course I went,' I say quietly. 'We were on the way back. Samson found it – the body.'

'Sorry,' says Dad, his voice softening. 'Come on, you – in the kitchen.' He helps me up gently by my elbow. 'Rescue Remedy and a mug of sweet tea. That's what you need. Good for shock. Then you can tell me all about it.'

I describe the whole experience as Dad listens and asks questions. I sip the too-sweet tea and start to feel better.

Later, I lie on my bed and message Kyle. '**Please call me – it's urgent!**'

I get no reply. I message Madz. '**Are you OK?**'

Her response is almost instant. '**No.**'

'**Want to come over?**'

'**No.**'

'**Still can't believe it,**' I reply. '**Call me if you want to talk.**'

I put my phone down on my bed and close my eyes. I feel so weird, wondering whose body it was, lying there.

In spite of all my worries, I'm nearly falling asleep when I hear a sound — a creak. I have this weird sensation as if someone's in the room with me. That's the scary thing when you can't see. For one wild moment I imagine that the killer had been watching me and followed me home . . .

'Joe! Is that you?' I demand crossly.

'Yeah.'

'You know you're supposed to knock and tell me it's you!' I yell, wide awake now. 'You gave me the fright of my life!'

'I thought you were asleep,' my brother says sheepishly, coming nearer so I can see the vague dark shape of him. 'I didn't want to wake you, only . . . Dad said you found a body!'

Joe sits on my bed and I tell him everything.

'What did it feel like — the finger?' he asks eagerly. 'Were you scared that whoever did it might still be around watching you?'

'That didn't occur to me, Joe — until just now when I thought *a stranger was in my room.*'

'Sorry 'bout that,' he says. 'Some watchdog, aren't you, Samson?'

I hear the thump of Samson's tail on the floor.

'Maybe they'll want to recruit him as a police dog now!' Joe says. 'Or you and Samson could become detectives. You know, investigate the crime – find out who did it.'

'Yeah, right,' I say, because how can a dog and girl who can't see solve a crime?

It's late when Mum gets home and I'm already in bed, but I can't sleep. I'm glad when she comes in, whispering, 'Libby, it's Mum. Are you awake?'

She sits on my bed and I tell the story all over again.

'And you called the police?' Mum asks.

'Yes, Madz was too upset.'

'Well done, my girl,' says Mum. 'I'm proud of you, holding it together and doing the right thing.'

I can't help smiling to myself. Typical Mum.

25

In the morning at breakfast time, Dad says, 'Are you OK to go to school on your own? I can take you and go in late, if you want me to.'

I'm puzzled, unsure why he's saying this. 'I'm OK.'

'Just be careful,' Dad says. 'Both of you. Stay on the busier roads. No alleyways. I don't want to scare you, but whoever killed that boy – they're still out there.'

'Dad!' says Joe. 'Give us a break. No one's going to attack us.'

'What I say, still stands,' says Dad. 'Just be careful.' He puts his arm round my shoulder and kisses me gently on the cheek.

When I arrive at school, Madz calls to me eagerly. 'It's all over the news, about your body!'

'Don't call it "my body"!' I protest. 'What does

the news say?'

'They've released his name,' she tells me. 'It's Zak Defoe.'

'Zak?' I repeat. One of the boys at the house in Harwell Heath was called Zak. It can't be him, can it?

'It says Zak was a model student,' Madz continues. 'He went to Grayson's – I've heard of that. It's not far from here. My mum's uncle used to teach there years ago. It costs loads. It says he was doing well, until he started skipping lessons. Then he ran away from home.'

Zak's not that uncommon a name. But he did have a posh voice. I noticed because he sounded different to the others. I start to feel sick.

'It's so sad, isn't it?' says Madz. 'When we found the body, it was just a body. But now he's a boy our age with a name. A boy who was alive, going to school, a boy with a mum who's grieving for him.'

'It's horrible to think about that,' I agree, swallowing hard.

Zak was the one who tried to give Kyle a knife. He seemed scared. The more I think about it, the more likely it seems that it is the same Zak. I need to do something – and I can't do it alone. Kyle has been gone for three days. I have to talk to someone. I have to tell Madz.

'Madz. I need your help,' I blurt out. 'I need to find Kyle – I think he's in danger. And I think I know where he is.'

'Where?' she asks.

'Harwell Heath,' I tell her. 'It's a village about an hour and a half away. We have to go on the train.'

'Is it something to do with this Zak? When exactly would we do this? And what danger is Kyle in?' The questions burst from Madz like fireworks.

I tell her everything – about the note from Charlie, how we've looked for him. All of it. When I've finished, Madz is silent. Her silence scares me. Is she going to lecture me and say we must go straight to the police? And I don't know – perhaps it's finally time I did?

'So if we go to this house in Harwell, how to do you think that will help?' she asks eventually.

'Kyle might be there, for a start,' I say. 'But even if he isn't, they may know where he is – and Charlie too. And after what happened to Zak – if it's the same Zak – then they may be more likely to tell us.'

'Or less,' Madz says, clearly not convinced. 'What

if the people in the house are involved? And Kyle – I know you like him, but how well do you really know him? He could have got drawn into something too. Do you think it's a gang thing?'

'I don't know what it is,' I admit, 'but I'm sure Kyle wouldn't get caught up in it. He's only trying to help Charlie. Listen – if we don't get anywhere, I promise I'll call the police.'

Madz sighs. 'OK, I'll come,' she says. 'Tomorrow?'

'Thanks, Madz! You're a good friend,' I tell her.

I wonder if she'll still feel like a good friend when she realises that I don't have the actual address of the house – Kyle had all the directions. I think I can remember though. And I'm hoping Samson will help too.

26

'Is this our train?' I ask Madz, as I hear one pull into the station. We're standing on the platform and we've been waiting ages because of train delays. I'm getting tetchy.

'What?' says Madz. 'Oh – yes. Come on.'

I'm always worried about the gap between the platform and the train and I'm relieved once we're safely on board. Madz finds us a group of four empty seats, with plenty of room for Samson to sit without being trodden on.

It's a bright sunny day but not as hot as it has been. Still, I pour some water carefully into Samson's bowl and take a few sips from my own bottle. Madz isn't as chatty as usual and seems a bit distracted.

'I don't know what I saw in Ollie,' she finally says. 'Now I look at him with Kayleigh, I wonder what on earth I was thinking.'

'You thought you liked him,' I tell her.

Madz sighs. 'I guess. He's so good-looking and popular. I never thought he'd be interested in someone like me – and I was right. He was using me.'

'You deserve better,' I tell her. 'It's his loss. *He* was lucky when you agreed to go out with him, not the other way round.'

She laughs. 'That's why I like you, Libs. You always say the right thing.'

Of course, I have no idea how good-looking Ollie is or not – or what that even means – but I know the way he speaks. I've always admired his confidence, but been less keen on what he says.

'He always sounded a bit up himself,' I admit.

'Why didn't you say something?' Madz exclaims.

'You'd never have listened,' I tell her. 'You'd have told me I was jealous.'

'Maybe,' she says. Then she asks, 'So what about Kyle?'

'We're not dating or anything like that,' I tell Madz, 'but I felt like there was something growing between us. We were going to go together back to the house in Harwell Heath – but then I got grounded.'

'Because of me,' Madz groans.

'You weren't to know what was going on.'

'Harwell Heath is the next stop,' says Madz. 'Oh — Harwell House is near here. My grandparents brought me here once.'

'I went with Kyle,' I say. 'Dad told you, didn't he?'

'He thought it was me. I was dead confused,' says Madz.

'I'm still sorry about that,' I tell her. 'I took some amazing photos there. Come on, Samson. We're getting off.'

'What's the address?' Madz asks as we get off the train and out of the station. 'I can get a route on my phone.'

It's the question I've been dreading. 'I don't have the actual address,' I tell her. 'Kyle did.'

'What?' she exclaims incredulously.

'I know the house is number five,' I say quickly. 'And I think I remember the route. But if we can't find it, the woman in the shop may remember. And Samson will help.'

'Libby! You're the one who's always telling me he doesn't know the way to places, and you have to tell him left and right,' Madz says with a snort. 'Now suddenly he comes with in-built maps?'

'I wish he did,' I say. Samson huffs. 'Don't worry,

Samson – I love you anyway.' I turn back to Madz. 'I know we started off heading right.'

She sighs. 'I guess we're here now, so we'll have to give it a go. At least I can use Google Maps to get us back to the station if we get lost.'

'We're not going to get lost,' I insist. 'It really isn't that far.'

We walk for a while. I remember the road went some way before coming to a crossroads.

'Is there a crossroads ahead?' I ask.

'Can't see one,' Madz tells me. She is walking in front, as there isn't room for her alongside Samson and me. 'Oh, actually, you might be right. There's something up ahead – yes – it's the end of the road. Now, left or right?'

'Left,' I say decisively, recognising the uneven narrow pavement. 'We should reach the shop in a couple of minutes.'

We do. Samson stops. I'm sure he remembers where we are, and remembers going inside. Though it might just be that he can smell food.

'Now there's a turning we need to take. I think it's the next one on the right,' I tell Madz. 'Can I go ahead with Samson? I think he might remember and automatically go the right way after that.'

'You hope!' says Madz, moving behind.

When we reach a turning, Samson doesn't seem keen to take it without instruction.

'His nose is definitely pointing down to the left,' says Madz.

'Left,' I tell Samson.

We take a few more turnings, using Samson's nose to judge it.

'Feel familiar?' Madz asks, hopefully.

'I think so,' I tell her. 'That's a post box, isn't it? It definitely feels right. The shapes of the hedges on the left and the shadowy large house shapes look right too. After these houses, are there some smaller, more modern ones? Maisonettes?'

'Looks like it,' she says.

'This is the road! Let me know when we get to number five.'

'I can see it now,' says Madz. 'It looks a bit run down. I wouldn't think anyone was living there from the outside.'

My skin's starting to prickle. 'I hope someone's in,' I say. I can sense Madz's unease and it's rubbing off on me.

'There's no bell. You want me to knock?'
'Yes – go on.'
She bangs three times and we wait.

27

'I don't think anyone's in,' says Madz after a tense couple of minutes.

I feel my whole body sag. 'I've dragged you all this way. What a waste of time.'

'Hang on,' she says. 'I'm wrong. I saw a shape moving through the glass. There's definitely someone in there.'

'Is anyone there?' I call, leaning towards the door. 'It's Libby here. I'm looking for Kyle.'

The voice on the other side makes me jump. 'You were looking for Charlie before, weren't you?'

'Is that Reuben?' I ask, though his childlike voice is so distinctive I am already certain it is. 'Do you think you could open the door?'

'Go away please. You can't come in.'

'I'm here with my friend Madz,' I explain. 'We're looking for Kyle *and* Charlie now. Have you seen them? Have they been here?'

'I'm not opening the door,' Reuben says firmly.

'Is something wrong?' I ask, hearing the tension in his voice. 'Has something happened?'

'It's dangerous. You should go home,' says Reuben.

'What's going on?' I ask him. 'We don't mean any harm. Is anyone there with you?'

Reuben's voice wobbles. 'I'm on my own. They've gone. They've all gone. My brothers left me and they're not coming back.'

'Why?' I ask. 'Why've they all gone?'

'They've gone,' Reuben repeats. 'They've gone – and . . .' His voice lowers to a whisper. 'Zak's dead.'

I feel myself swaying as I remember the feel of the finger, the hand, the arm in the grass in the alley – the stiffness. Then I think of the voice of the same boy who stood at this door when I was here last time, saying he wished he had people that cared enough to come looking for him.

It *was* him. It was Zak's body we found. The boy who spoke to us here last week.

Dead.

'They're all scared now,' Reuben continues, his voice low. 'They've all gone. I wanted them to stay.

I liked having my brothers here with me. We had pizza. Jez gave me Heroes. They're my favourite chocolates. But now he's gone. And they didn't even clean up – they left a big mess. I wanted to go with them, but they said no.'

'I'm so sorry,' I tell him. 'Please, can you let us in? Maybe we can help you.'

'You can't help me. And you can't come in. I told you to go home.'

'Could you just open the door a little?' Madz suggests. 'We won't come in, but it'll be easier to talk.'

'Is this a trick?' Reuben asks suspiciously.

'Of course not,' I tell him. 'Maybe instead of us coming in, you could come out and talk to us?'

'I'm not meant to talk to anyone,' says Reuben. 'They said I mustn't.'

At that moment, Samson gives a loud snort. He's getting impatient on the doorstep and is keen to either get inside or move on.

'Did you bring your dog?' Reuben asks, suddenly sounding more animated.

'Yes,' I tell him. 'Samson's here.'

I hear a click as the door opens, but it must be

just a crack because the shapes and shadows haven't changed.

'Can I stroke him?' Reuben asks. 'I like dogs.'

'Yes,' I say. 'Thank you for asking first. People don't always do that. Sit, Samson. Reuben wants to stroke you.'

The shadows move this time and then I see the shape of Reuben's arm and his body bending down to Samson.

'Hi, I'm Madz,' says Madz. 'We're just looking for Kyle – and Charlie.'

'You're a lovely dog,' Reuben tells Samson.

'Madz is my friend,' I explain, aware that Reuben seems to have blanked her – though of course he may have smiled at her. I can't tell.

'I think he likes me!' says Reuben.

'I think he does,' I agree, as Samson wriggles round closer to Reuben. 'Reuben, are you OK? Do you have anyone to help you now your brothers have gone?'

'They said they were my brothers – my friends,' says Reuben. 'But your friends don't just stay in your house for weeks and then go away and leave you with all the mess, do they?'

'No, that's awful,' I tell him. 'Were Kyle and Charlie your brothers too? Or just Jez and Zak?'

'Not Charlie and Kyle. But they were here on Thursday. They didn't live here. Well, Charlie did for a bit. Mainly it was Jez and Zak, and Marty sometimes. Zak's dead. Jerome and Marty have gone.'

'And what about Kyle and Charlie? Where did they go?' I ask.

'I don't know.'

'Did you speak to them?'

'Yes but I shouldn't of. Jez told me I shouldn't of.'

'So do you have any idea where Kyle or Charlie are now?'

'No.' He says this so quickly that I'm not sure I believe him.

'Shall we go, Libby?' Madz asks quietly.

'What did you say?' Reuben demands. 'Are you whispering about me?'

'No,' says Madz. 'Not at all. It's kind of you to come out and talk to us.'

'I like Samson. He's so soft,' says Reuben.

'Do you think Kyle and Charlie are in danger?' I ask him.

'Maybe,' he says, nonchalantly. 'They might be

188

dead. Like Zak.'

'Do you know who killed Zak?' I ask.

'No,' says Reuben. 'You're asking a lot of questions.'

'If Charlie and Kyle are alive, we want to help them. Maybe you can help,' I say. I'm getting frustrated now. Reuben is our last hope. 'I have some treats for Samson,' I tell him. 'Would you like to give him one?'

'Oh yes!' says Reuben.

I unzip a pocket in my bag and pull out a pack of treats. 'Just give him one,' I tell Reuben, holding it out towards him.

Reuben laughs, after a moment. 'Oh! He licked my hand! It tickled!'

'Is there anything at all that you know that might help us?' I ask him. I'm trying not to sound too desperate.

'Charlie was talking about mints again,' says Reuben. 'He must of run out. He said "lots of mints". He said it to Kyle when Jez and Marty weren't there. I wanted to ask if I could have mints too. I like mints. But I wasn't meant to be listening.'

'I'm not sure mints will help us find them,' says

Madz. 'Though thanks for telling us. Really we really need an address, or a place.'

'That's all I know,' says Reuben. 'You need to go now.'

'Are you OK?' I ask him, realising he didn't answer when I asked before. 'Do you have any family – anyone who helps you?' I'm feeling bad at the thought of leaving him on his own.

'I've got Shareen. Do you think I should call her? She's my social worker, but my brothers told me to tell her I was ill 'cos they didn't want her coming round.'

'I think you should call her,' says Madz.

'Yes, that sounds like a good idea,' I tell him. 'Do you have food and stuff like that?'

'Oh yes. I go shopping at the shop.'

'Good,' I say. 'We'd better go now. Thanks for talking to us.'

'Yeah, thanks,' says Madz.

'Bye Samson, good dog!' says Reuben. Then I hear the door close.

28

'Poor Reuben,' I say as we walk back towards the station.

'Poor us too,' says Madz. 'Standing on the doorstep all that time and we got no useful info at all.'

'But they just took over his place, scrounged off him and then abandoned him,' I point out. 'One of them must've decided Reuben's place would be a good place to live.'

'You're too caring,' says Madz. 'I think you should leave Kyle and Charlie to sort themselves out. "Lot of mints"!' she adds. 'Really helpful, that.'

'They weren't talking about mints – unless it's a slang word for drugs or something?' I say, thinking. 'It can't be a place, can it? Although some of the villages round here have weird names . . .'

'A place called Lotofmints?' Madz laughs.

'Hang on.' My mind is whirring. Something Gran said. What was it? Then I remember. 'What about *allotments*?' I ask. 'Could he have misheard?'

'Allotments? Like those little gardens people have to grow stuff? Why would they want one of those?'

'Could they be growing drugs?' I ask. 'Like cannabis or something?'

Madz is silent for a moment. 'I think that needs light and heat. I don't think you can grow it outside, but I'm no expert.'

'I wonder if there are any allotments near here? Might be worth a try,' I suggest.

'We could ask in the shop, I guess,' says Madz.

'Hello,' says the woman in the shop. 'You back again? Did you find the boy you were looking for?'

'We found the house where he was staying,' I tell her, 'but he's not there any more. Are there any allotments near here?'

'Allotments? Edge of Gretan – that's the nearest town. You know it?'

'It was the stop before this on the train,' says Madz.

'Yes, that's right,' says the woman. 'Well not far from the station there's allotments. You turn right out of the station and keep going and you'll come to them on the left.'

'Thank you so much,' I say. I wonder if we ought to buy something, but Madz is already walking towards the door.

'I suppose you want to go there now?' Madz says when we're outside.

'It is on the way back,' I point out.

'And you think we'll find them just standing around by the allotments, or busy with their watering cans?' Madz huffs. 'We don't even know it was allotments he was talking about.'

'Let's just look. Please?' I beg. 'It can't do any harm.'

Madz sighs. 'OK, OK. We'll go there.'

She's quiet on the walk back to the station.

'Thanks for coming with me,' I say to her.

'I know you're worried about Kyle,' she says. 'I understand. But one boy has been *stabbed*. Do you trust him, Libby? If it's something to do with drugs, do you think he and Charlie are in it together?'

'Kyle wouldn't get involved in that. He only wanted to help Charlie,' I insist.

With Madz's help we catch the train towards home and get off after one stop. She finds the allotments easily.

'There's a gate and a bunch of sheds,' Madz tells me. I hear the gate rattling as she tries it. 'It's locked. I guess just the people with allotments have a key.'

Samson shifts impatiently by my legs, wondering what we are doing.

'Can you see through the gates?' I ask. 'Is anyone around?'

'I can see,' says Madz. 'It's divided into rectangles with vegetables growing and some of them have sheds. There's a few people right at the back digging and watering. Believe me – Kyle and Charlie aren't going to be here.'

'Is there a wall round it, or a fence?' I ask, aware of the high dark blur each side of the gate.

'Fence,' says Madz. 'Why, you planning to climb over?'

'Don't be daft! Maybe there's a gap somewhere?'

'You don't give up, do you?' she says.

'It's just – we've come all this way . . .' I stop speaking. I can hear something. 'Hang on – I can hear voices,' I whisper. 'There's people talking. Can you see where?'

'I told you there were a few people there,' says Madz. 'They're not together though – I can't see who's talking.'

The voices continue. We both listen.

'I think they're in one of the sheds,' says Madz. 'There's a shed door partly open in the plot on the far right – but I can't see in.'

I listen. I can't catch the actual dialogue, but the voices are male – and young. The conversation sounds serious – not larking about, no laughter. Then I hear name 'Zak'. My skin prickles.

'Did you hear that?' I whisper to Madz.

'What?'

'Zak – he said Zak. I think it's them, or someone who knows them. Jez or Marty – or Charlie and Kyle. I can't tell.'

I strain to listen harder. I hear the words: 'It's no use.' The grainy voice . . . sounds like Charlie. It really does.

Samson gives a low growl. I feel him tense.

'What's up with Samson?' I ask Madz.

Madz sounds nervous. 'There's a woman coming this way. She's got a dog – a bigger dog than Samson. She looks like she can hardly control it.'

I step between Samson and the gate, to shield him. It's instinctive. The dog barks as its shape comes into my vision. Samson barks back.

The woman and dog have passed, but I hear a voice from the other side of the gate, closer than the shed. Whoever it is – they've come out.

'It's just someone with a dog out there,' says the voice, much closer now. The gravelly, familiar tone shakes me. The voice that called my name on the path. It's Charlie – I'm sure it is.

I am so stunned to actually find him, I can't speak.

29

'Charlie?' I call gently.

'Who's that?' His voice is sharp, nervous.

'It's me – Libby,' I say. 'And Madz is here too – from school.'

'What the . . . ?' The voice comes closer. 'Are you crazy? How the heck did you find us?'

'I was looking for you with Kyle after I gave him the note. But now he's missing too. You said you were in danger. I wanted to help.'

'Ky?' says Charlie angrily. 'I know you said Libby was helping you, but did you tell her we were here?'

'Kyle!' I cry. 'Is Kyle there too?'

'Yes. I can't believe he told you. He's a grass!'

'No, Charlie!' My voice is a squeal. 'It wasn't Kyle who told me.'

'We worked it out from something Reuben said,' Madz explains. 'We found this place on our own.'

'Kyle hasn't been in touch all week,' I say. 'Kyle! Kyle! Tell him, will you?'

'Keep your voice down!' Charlie hisses. 'You never know who's watching. Come with me. You'd better both get in here before someone spots you. That dog of yours stands out a mile. There's a gap a bit further along.'

'Come on,' says Madz. 'This way – I've found it.'

She guides Samson and me through the gap in the fence and I stumble over tree roots on the other side. Madz leads me towards the sheds.

'Libby,' says Kyle. 'I'm sorry.'

'I was so worried about you!' I tell him, my heart pounding. He reaches out and takes my hand.

'Mind the step,' he says, as my foot finds it. 'Come in here, out of sight.'

The shed is dark and hot, with an earthy, mushroomy smell. There's not much space and my arm brushes what feels like the handle of a large spade.

'Here,' says Kyle. 'There's a couple of crates – perch on this one.'

I sit down gingerly. Samson sits upright beside me.

'I'm sorry, Libby,' says Kyle. 'I had to switch

my phone off so no one could locate me. It was too dangerous.'

'But you found Charlie!'

'Yes. He was at the house in Harwell Heath. It was incredible timing because he wasn't staying.'

'So can't you come home?' I ask. 'Both of you?'

'No,' says Kyle. 'It's not that simple. How did you find us? No one knows we're here. Not even Reuben.'

'Yeah – I'd like to hear this,' says Charlie.

Madz and I do our best to explain. Charlie laughs at the 'lots of mints' clue.

'Good old Reuben,' he says. 'But we'll have to move on now. He might go blabbing to someone else too. And it's nice of you to want to help, but what exactly do you think you can do? Unless you can get hold of a lot of cash quick? You got any savings?'

'Charlie!' Kyle exclaims. 'You can't go raiding their savings.'

'What's the problem?' I ask. 'Why do you need money? Tell me. I want to understand.'

'It started a couple of months back,' said Charlie, sighing. 'My mate offered me a job – delivering and that. I was just taking stuff place to place. Packages.'

'Drugs,' says Kyle.

'Yeah, but I never knew that – not at first,' says Charlie. 'Jez was a good mate. He paid me and he got me somewhere to stay. He gave me a phone and stuff. These trainers. I know I was stupid. But I owed money already so it seemed like a way out. Then I got robbed – guy on a bike jumped me and nicked the stuff. I took a beating trying to stop him, but he still got it.'

'So what happened?' I ask.

'I went back to Jez. I thought he'd understand. He'd see I'd been attacked. I mean, what was I meant to do? But he said that package was worth loads – a grand or something. I had no idea. He said I had to earn it back or Marty would kill me. I know Jez is under pressure from Marty – he's in charge. So he's making me sell stuff on the street to get the money back, but it's taking forever. It's dangerous. I don't want to do it any more. I want out. He was threatening me and I said I needed more time – but time ran out yesterday. If Marty finds me, I'm dead.'

'Surely the police could help you?' I say.

Charlie laughs bitterly. 'I've been dealing drugs.

I'm a kid from a referral unit. I'm trouble. Why would they believe me? And even if they did, they'd still arrest me. There's no way out. Marty'll find me – him and his mates. They've got contacts, even in prison. Jez said they'll kill me and they mean it. I know they mean it. A mate of mine got done in last week. I dunno what happened, but I know he wanted out too. He'd had enough.'

'Zak?' I ask, suddenly feeling sick.

'Yes,' says Kyle. 'We met him at the house. He's dead, Libby.'

'I found his body. Well, Samson did,' I tell them.

'You what?' says Kyle, and I explain what happened.

'I saw the body,' says Madz. 'It was awful. And you say they killed him just because he wanted to get out?'

'Looks like it,' says Charlie. 'And I'll be next.'

'So what's the answer?' I demand. 'What are you going to do?'

'I dunno. I've stuffed it all up. I'm a loser. That's just what I am.'

'There must be a way out,' I say.

'I'm in too deep,' says Charlie. 'You wanna

know what I did?'

'Tell us,' says Madz.

'I needed to sell more, quicker. So I went to a place where I thought there'd be buyers. Only I was down the wrong end, and it was outside Marty's territory. I was stupid. I didn't realise that territory was Nat's – he's from a rival gang. Nat went mental. Sent his crew after me. They want to kill me now and all. And Marty found out, so he thinks I've been working for Nat instead of him!'

My head is spinning. 'You *have* to go to the police.'

'No way,' says Charlie.

'I said I'd find Marty,' says Kyle. 'Explain that Charlie made a mistake. That all he was doing was trying to get the money back to give him.'

'That's too dangerous, Kyle,' I protest. 'There must be another way. Or somewhere Charlie can go to stay safe? Charlie, how about your dad?'

'That loser?' Charlie chips in, his voice full of hate. 'He's not my real dad, didn't you know?'

'It's your real dad that I'm talking about,' I tell him.

'How d'you know about that?' says Charlie.

'I didn't get a chance to tell you,' says Kyle.

'Hassan told us about your dad. Libby and I – we talked to Tia and your mum. We've got his name. Your birth dad.'

'I know his name,' says Charlie. 'I went through my mum's stuff and found it. But much use that is. There's thousands of Johnny Hunters.'

'But your mum found a photo,' I tell Charlie. 'And my brother helped me. He used an app to find a match for the photo online. And I've got an email address for your real dad's work. I'll find it for you.'

'Really?' says Charlie, in surprise. 'You sure it's him?'

'Definitely,' I say.

'That's amazing, Libby!' says Kyle. 'I wish I'd thought of doing that.'

'Look,' I say. I rummage around in my bag and find the scrap of paper where Joe had written it. 'And I can show you the photo too.' I open pictures on my phone.

'That's my dad?' Charlie's voice is strange – soft, vulnerable. But he doesn't sound shocked. He obviously isn't connecting this face with the man in the car five years ago.

'He's in Birmingham. Maybe he can help you,' I suggest.

'But he never wanted me,' says Charlie. 'He didn't stick around when I was born, did he? He might be no better than Vince. I've been let down so much, I don't think I can cope with any more.'

'He did want you,' I tell him. 'He wanted to marry your mum. She told us, didn't she, Kyle?'

'She did,' says Kyle.

'I could do with a full-time dad now. An overtime dad,' says Charlie. His voice is gravelly. 'But look at me. Even if I find him, he'll run a mile, I'm sure.'

'He might, but I don't think so,' I tell him.

'How do you know?' says Charlie.

I hesitate. 'Tell him, Kyle,' I say. 'It's your story to tell.'

'Yes,' says Kyle. 'You remember that time when we were at primary and that man got us in that car?'

'How could I forget?' says Charlie. 'What's that got to do with anything?'

'His face stayed in my mind – like it was imprinted,' says Kyle. 'Then, when your mum found this picture of your dad, I recognised him. It's the same guy. One hundred per cent.'

'You what?'

'And I didn't know what to make of it,' Kyle continues. 'Libby reckons he got us in that car because he'd been watching you. He wanted to get to know his son, spend time with you. Then it all went wrong. He realised he should never have done that – offered us a lift, like that. You got me out and we ran off. And he couldn't talk to your mum after that, ask for contact, could he? But he did want to know you.'

'That was my dad?' Charlie speaks in a whisper.

'Yes,' I tell him. 'And he does care, see?'

'It took me a while to get my head round it,' says Kyle.

'That's like – so crazy,' says Charlie.

'It's true though,' says Kyle. 'I'm sure it's true. You could email him, and just see what happens.'

'Yeah,' says Charlie. 'I guess I could.'

He sounds so wistful, I feel like crying. I wish his dad would just tap on this shed door and tell Charlie he loves him and he's going to rescue him and take him far away from all this and look after him.

There's a sudden rustle in the bushes – and the door bursts open.

'Well well well.'

It's a man's voice. At first I think it's the police, but I'm wrong.

'So this is where you've been hanging out. Got visitors, have you?'

30

Light comes into the shed as the door is pulled wide open. I shield my eyes with one hand, resting the other protectively on Samson. Then most of the light is blocked by a big shape in the doorway.

'They just turned up. I . . . I don't know how they found me,' says Charlie. My skin prickles when I hear the fear in his wavering voice.

'A blind girl managed to find you?' the voice says scornfully. 'Don't seem like you was that well hidden then, does it?'

'And you – how . . . how did you find us?' Charlie asks.

'Woman in the village shop. I went in for a can and heard her nattering. Telling her mate about a girl with a guide dog, looking for a boy and now looking for the allotments. Reubs mentioned a guide dog a while back, so I put two and two together. Easy, eh? There's no hiding from me.'

'We'll go,' says Madz. 'We don't mean any harm.'

'Oh no you won't,' says the man.

'Marty, please – just let them go. They don't know anything . . .' Charlie sounds terrified. I shudder. I feel Madz's hand clutching mine.

'We'll go – please,' I say. 'We don't want to bother you.'

'No, you're right,' he sneers. 'You won't bother me – because you're going to help me.'

I feel instantly wobbly and reach for the wall of the shed to keep my balance. I flinch as a splinter pierces the skin on my finger, but I don't move. There's something about his voice. He scares me. I wonder if it was him that killed Zak.

'Help you?' I repeat.

'Yeah – I think you girls would be perfect for this. Won't they, Chaz?'

'Can't you just . . .' I hear Charlie begin to reply. I'm hoping he's going to tell Marty to leave us be and let us go. But his voice peters out. He's too scared and I don't blame him.

'Help you how?' asks Madz quietly.

'Nothing major,' says Marty. 'Just take a package – deliver it for us. You can do that. I've seen how good you are at finding your way around.'

'You want us to deliver drugs for you?' I ask in a whisper.

'I never said that, did I? It's a package. Best not to ask about the contents,' he says. 'Just take it — done, end of.'

'There's no need for this,' says Kyle, quietly. 'Charlie just wants to get the money back for you that he owes, that's all.'

'And he's made a right mess of it,' Marty snaps.

'Let me do it,' says Kyle. 'Not the girls. I'll do it instead.'

'You? And who the heck are you?'

'Kyle. I just wanted to help Charlie.'

'What, help him hide out here? Keep him cooped up safe when he's meant to be working? There's feds sniffing around since that kid got shanked last week, and I bet there's some looking for you and all. I don't want us getting busted. But who's gonna suspect these two? Girl with guide dog plus friend? You look clean as fresh snow, don't you? That's the beauty!' He laughs — but his laugh sounds evil to me.

'We don't want to get involved,' I beg. 'We just want to go. I promise we won't come back — we'll stay right out of it.'

'No, this needs doing, and you're gonna to do it.'

'What if we don't?' Madz asks bravely.

'Just do it,' Charlie says quickly, before Marty has a chance to answer. 'It'll be OK. Just don't argue or ask questions.'

'Good advice, Chaz,' says Marty. 'You got them involved so it's you that's gonna suffer if they don't do what they're told. That's fair, innit Chaz? And you don't wanna see him dead, and your friend Kyle here – do you, girls? You don't want to be responsible for that, eh?'

I gulp. 'Please – it's not their fault we came looking for them.'

'Shut it,' Marty hisses, and his voice is so scary, I do. I can feel Samson bristling beside me, shifting his paws. He gives a low growl, a sound I've never heard from him before.

'I'm gonna slip this in your bag,' Marty tells me, ignoring Samson. 'You won't even have to touch it or think about it. And you're gonna remember this address. You take it. Only two stops down the line. Give it to Ron. Right, I'm off. Things to do, people to see, you know?'

I wait. None of us move. I think we're alone again, but I'm not completely sure. 'Has he gone?' I whisper.

'Yeah,' says Kyle.

I crouch down, hugging Samson, who snuggles against me and licks my face.

'What are we going to do?' Madz asks.

'Do what he said,' says Charlie. 'Just do it. Just go, Libby.'

'OK,' I say. 'Come on, Madz. Walk, Samson.'

I'm shaking as Samson pulls the harness and Madz walks beside me. She squeezes my hand, but doesn't speak again until we're a few streets away.

'It'll be OK, Libs,' Madz says. Her voice sounds panicky. 'We'll just take this straight to the police. Let them deal with it all.'

'But he's threatening to kill Charlie and Kyle – didn't you hear?' I snap. 'I reckon he means it. He might've murdered Zak. We have to do what Marty said. We deliver the package and then we stay well away.'

When we're off the train and we've walked for five minutes, Madz stops outside a house and says this is

211

the address. We're both quiet for a moment.

'Are you going to ring the bell?' I ask.

'I'm scared,' says Madz. 'We're doing something illegal. Something serious.'

'Keep your voice down!' I tell her. 'It's not as if Marty gave us much choice.'

'Isn't that what they all say?' asks Madz. 'Someone else told me to do it. Does that make it OK?'

'Ring the bell!' I demand, not wanting to think about it. I only want it to be over – the package is burning an even bigger hole in my bag than the note Charlie gave me. I feel a clenching in my chest.

The ding-dong of the bell brings me back to the present. I wait, tense until the shadows form as the door opens.

'Yeah?' says a voice.

'Are you Ron?' Madz asks.

'Who wants to know?' says the voice.

'Marty sent us,' says Madz.

'You got something for me?' the voice asks.

'It's in here,' I say, reaching into my bag. I hold out the package and feel it pulled from my grasp.

'Ta,' says the voice. 'Wait – I got something for you an' all.'

'We don't want anything. We have to go,' I say anxiously.

'No, Marty called me. I've had clear instructions. When you turn up, I'm to give you this. Take it to him. He'll be waiting on the industrial estate near the allotments. Tatewell Warehouses – number six.'

My heart sinks into my sandals. 'He didn't say there would be anything to go back,' I plead. 'He just said to bring this to you.'

'Well, I got something he needs,' says the man, 'and you guys are great little couriers. You'll be rewarded, fair and square.'

'We don't want rewards,' says Madz. 'We just want to go home.'

'So you'd put your friends in danger?' he says.

'No, of course not,' I say quickly.

'Won't take you more than an hour and then you can go home. So go now and get on with it. I'll let him know you're on your way.'

The door slams shut.

'Come on,' says Madz wearily. 'He might be watching from the window.'

'Walk, Samson,' I instruct, and I feel the gentle, reassuring pull of the harness as he does.

'We can't do this,' whispers Madz after a minute or two. 'We must go to the police.'

'I'm scared,' I tell her. 'What if we do and something happens to Kyle and Charlie? And remember what Marty said. He threatened us too.'

'Are you suggesting we take it then?' Madz asks.

'Just this once. If he tries to make us do anything else, we just go to the police anyway,' I tell her.

'OK. But no more,' Madz agrees. 'I'm not doing this again.'

31

Madz is unusually quiet on the journey. When we get off the train, I feel like I can hear my heart pounding in my ears with each step. We walk along the road, Samson panting as we go. I wonder if we should stop to give him some water, but Madz wants to get this over with first.

'Here's the warehouse,' Madz says after a few minutes. 'Oh – I can see him. He's waiting outside. Come on.'

'Well, hello,' Marty sneers. 'Come inside, girls – you never know who might be watching.'

I was hoping we'd just hand him the package and leave, but before I know what's happening Madz is leading Samson and me into a building. The sounds of our footsteps echo on the concrete floor and I sense this warehouse is big. It's dark too, with light only at the far end where the windows must be.

My mind slips back to Charlie. I thought Marty

was going to let us go, but maybe he has other plans. Maybe he needs to be sure we keep quiet. I try to push away the scary thought that enters my mind. He isn't going to kill us, is he?

'You've done well,' Marty says. 'Here's a little thank you.'

'What is it?' Madz asks.

'Open it,' says Marty. He's clearly given her something. I hope it isn't drugs.

'What is it?' I ask.

'Money,' says Madz in wonder. 'It must be fifty quid in here.'

'We don't want your money!' I exclaim, turning to face Marty. But his vague shape has moved, and when I turn again I see he's standing nearer to Madz.

'Bit ungrateful, aren't you?' Marty sounds surprised, but I'm not sure if it's real surprise or pretend.

'We didn't do it for money,' says Madz.

Marty laughs. 'You did it for *lurvvve* then, did you?'

'No!' Madz says firmly. 'We helped you out, but we just want to go now.'

'Yes,' I agree. 'Please – can we just go?'

'So you don't care about your mates then?' says

Marty. 'You don't care what happens to them?'

'Of course we do.'

'You want to see them?'

'Where are they?' Madz asks.

'I'll show you,' says Marty.

I grasp Madz's arm. I have an uneasy feeling. More than uneasy – terrified. Has he killed them?

'Just through here,' Marty says.

Madz gasps. But I can see nothing. We've been led into a room to one side of the warehouse, but there's barely any light in here. I don't like it. I want to get out. I pull back.

'What?' I whisper to Madz.

'They're tied up on chairs, and gagged,' she says quietly.

My stomach lurches and I put my hand over it protectively. 'You can't do this. Let them go!' I demand.

'No,' he says, his voice curdled with threat.

Marty's right in front of me now – so close I almost jump. For the first time, I can just about make out his face. The whites of his eyes look large, like boiled eggs, but scary. Everything's spinning. This can't be happening. I've lost my bearings – I'm not

217

even sure which way the door is. I feel a tug from Samson. I'm sure he understands. My arm touches something and I realise it's a square metal post, going from the floor to the ceiling. I rest my hand against it.

'We did what you asked,' says Madz desperately. 'You can't do this to them.'

'I can do exactly what I like,' Marty says. 'And if you want me to let them go, it's in your hands. You're good workers, I've seen that. Quick and efficient. And no chance of arousing suspicion. You're perfect. You earn the cash back for me that Chaz here managed to lose me, and then you can all go home. You can take the money I offered, or leave it. That's up to you. All right?'

'No!' Madz shouts.

'You said we could go after the first package,' I remind Marty, stepping back from him. 'We did you a favour and brought one back too, which wasn't part of the deal.'

'I don't think you get how this works.' For some reason, Marty's voice is even more threatening when he speaks softly than when he is loud. 'I give the orders and you follow them. I'm the boss, get it? But you can have it your way if you like. I'll cut their throats right now.'

Madz gasps. 'No – please. Put that away!' I catch the glint of metal and know he has a knife. I can hear muffled noises and what sounds like chairs scraping on the ground – Charlie and Kyle can clearly see this too.

'You just take this one for me and that'll be your lot, I promise,' says Marty. 'I'm a man of my word.'

'You're not,' I say, and instantly regret my words as I feel his finger touch my cheek. I jerk back, letting go of the post. I can't bear him touching me. He's moved again, but now I'm not sure where. I turn – and he's there in front of me again.

Samson shuffles anxiously against my legs. He gives a low growl and then barks. The bark echoes in the cavernous space. He can sense Marty is a threat. I wish Samson could protect me, leap in and attack Marty, but guide dogs are chosen for their placid, non-aggressive nature and Samson is the gentlest of gentle dogs.

'Shut it, dog!' Marty's voice is callous. Samson suddenly yelps in pain. My heart lurches.

'Don't!' Madz cries. 'Leave Samson alone!'

'No!' I yell, unsure if Marty's kicked him or

stabbed him. 'No!' I drop the harness and lead, so that Samson can get away if Marty goes for him again. 'Please! We'll do what you say. Just tell us where to go.'

'That's better,' Marty huffs. 'You've seen sense. Here's the stuff. Look after it,' he adds quietly. 'This is valuable. Very valuable.'

His shape blurs across my vision as he hands the package to Madz. Then he steps back. There's a clang, and a strange grunt. I hear a thud. I can't see Marty now at all.

'What's happened?' I cry. 'What's he done? Is it Samson?'

Madz is breathing fast and loud beside me. 'Marty just knocked himself out on that post. Hurry – we've got to help the boys before he comes round.'

'What? How?' I turn to Madz in confusion. Samson's warm side brushes against my legs. I stroke him in relief and reach for the harness, but I can't find the lead and Samson seems stuck. His lead is caught in something.

'Samson,' Madz says. She sounds a little wild. 'He didn't know what to do when you let him go and when Marty stepped back his foot caught in Samson's lead. He went flying – hit his head on that post. Let me untangle the lead. We need to be quick!'

'Oh Samson!' I say. 'You good boy!'

He slaps his tail against me, though I'm sure he's no idea what he did. I feel the lead slacken and find the end. Madz has freed it.

'Come on!' Madz pulls me by the hand towards the chairs where the boys are tied. 'You untie Kyle.' She guides my hand to the back of the chair. I feel up towards Kyle's head and untie the gag first, my hand shaking.

'Ta!' he says, coughing.

I move on to his hands. The rope's tied tight. I'm struggling to do it, but then suddenly it loosens and he's free. Kyle unties his feet himself. He squeezes my hand.

'You done it?' Charlie's voice. He's already out of his chair. 'We gotta to run before Marty comes round.'

'Madz!' I call.

'I'm here. Don't worry – let Kyle guide you.'

I feel Kyle's hand touch mine and I reach for his arm.

'This way,' he says.

'Hup hup!' I tell Samson and I hold tight to Kyle's arm as we run. Samson is reluctant at first, but finally starts running with us.

'Mind the step!' Kyle yells as we burst out through a doorway and into the bright sunlight.

32

'Let's just get a bit further away,' Kyle says, 'then we can stop for a breath.'

Samson doesn't seem to mind that we're going much faster than usual. I'm terrified that I'm going to trip, but he still guides me carefully, even though Marty's kick must have scared him.

'Oh Samson,' I say, once we've stopped. 'You saved us!' I throw my arms around him. 'I love you,' I tell him, hugging him tighter. 'You're my hero.'

'What do we do now?' Madz pants. 'I've still got the package. I didn't know whether to drop it – I didn't have time to think.'

'We have to call the police,' I tell her. 'How bad do you think Marty was? Should we call an ambulance too?'

'I'm sorry I got you into this,' says Charlie. 'I'm so sorry – but I'm gonna head off now. The police – they won't believe anything I say. I wanna get out of trouble, not into it.'

'But Charlie . . .' I say.

'He's gone,' says Madz. 'Running fast too.'

'You're not going to run off, are you?' I ask Kyle, squeezing his arm tight.

'I'm staying with you, don't worry,' says Kyle. 'When Marty threatened us with a knife and tied us up, I thought I was dead. He said if we fought back, he'd kill the two of you. You've just saved my life.' His voice is full of emotion.

'I'm calling the police,' says Madz. 'But one of you can speak to them. I'll only get all tongue-tied.'

'We should tell them everything we know and let them sort it out,' I say. 'Including Reuben. I'm still worried about him.'

Madz gets through and hands the phone to me. I answer the questions as best I can, though I hand the phone back to Madz to describe Marty. We're told to stay where we are. An ambulance is on its way and the police are coming too. They seem especially interested to hear that we still have the package. Madz says she's put it in her bag. I take the chance to give Samson a drink of water.

When the police come, they tell us the warehouse

is empty. Marty's gone, but there's a trail of blood. Then they say they'll take us to the police station and that they'll have to call our parents.

'My mum will go crazy,' Madz groans.

I don't like to think how my parents will react. They probably won't let me out without a chaperone for another ten years.

We are interviewed separately. Mum's in Dublin at a conference, so it's Dad who sits beside me. He squeezes my hand gently, but I can tell he's angry by the little huffs he's giving when he breathes. He's assuming it's all some kind of mistake, and that I have nothing to do with anything. I wish he didn't have to be here while I answer these questions.

The room is small and my voice seems to bounce loudly off the walls. There's no natural light and I just want to get out and go home. I'm scared I'm going to get arrested for trafficking drugs. I wonder if I'd be allowed to have Samson with me in prison. I push away this thought, but it's comforting to have Samson under the chair with me now. Once I start talking, I tell the police everything – from Charlie and the note, to my outings with Kyle, the house in Harwell Heath – and the packages.

My dad keeps trying to interrupt, and the policewoman interviewing has to stop him. 'My daughter can't see. She can't have had any idea there were drugs involved!' he insists.

'Please, sir!' DC Fenn interrupts. 'If you carry on like this, we'll have to ask you to leave and get another responsible adult instead.'

'Apologies,' says Dad, and I can hear him taking deep breaths to calm down. 'This is just hard to take in.'

'I do understand, sir. But we are grateful to your daughter for helping us with our enquiries. She's providing very useful information. So Libby,' she continues to me, 'tell me about Kyle. How well do you know him?'

I tell her about school and art and our trip to Harwell Heath. She asks more questions which I can't answer, like where he has been for the last few days and where he lives.

'I'm sure that it was Marty who killed that boy Zak,' I add. 'He was the boss. They were all scared of him, and he threatened to slit Kyle and Charlie's throats. *And* he kicked Samson. Have you found him yet?'

'We're still looking for him, and Charlie and the other boy, Jerome – or Jez, I believe he calls himself,' says DC Fenn.

'Charlie didn't do anything,' I tell her. 'He's just scared to talk to you.'

'Well once we find him, he can explain, can't he?' she says.

'And Reuben?' I ask. 'Will you send someone to help Reuben? It can't be his fault that he got involved. I'm sure he had no idea what was going on.'

'Yes, of course. It sounds like he was cuckooed.'

'Cuckooed?' Dad repeats.

'This is what happens with county lines,' DC Fenn explains. 'A gang sets up a line – a phone number – and they recruit kids to move drugs around the country. Then they find someone vulnerable and take over their home. Like cuckoos laying eggs in another bird's nest. The kids stay there. Sometimes it's a vulnerable drug user, sometimes a lonely older person or someone with learning difficulties – like Reuben.'

'Poor Reuben,' I say. 'He thought they were his friends. He called them his brothers. He was really upset that they'd all gone and left him.'

227

'They were just using him,' says DC Fenn. 'Don't worry, we'll make sure it doesn't happen to him again. We can put a closure order on his property to prevent anyone going in who shouldn't be there, and we'll check that he has the support he needs.'

'And these kids they've got involved with – they're just kids?' says Dad. 'Surely they don't set out to become drug dealers.'

'The gang leaders groom them,' DC Fenn explains. 'The drug dealer acts like a friend and buys the young person things – mobile phones, trainers. And after a while they offer them the chance to make some money – tell them it's a job, as a courier. They start delivering packages and they get paid and they're happy. The dealers get them transporting drugs from towns and cities to villages, and they give them somewhere to stay too. It's hard for us to track them across different regions.'

'That's pretty much how Charlie described it,' I comment.

'Next thing they know, they're caught up in it,' says DC Fenn. 'They're expected to bring the money in. And if they don't do what they're told, they find their new friends suddenly get a lot less friendly.

They use violence and threats. And if one or two get killed along the way or end up in prison, the dealers couldn't care less because they're easily replaced. A lot of kids are vulnerable and get hooked in.'

'What a dreadful business,' says Dad.

'Sometimes the gang leader arranges for the kid to be robbed and then says he owes the money he's lost and that way he's trapped,' DC Fenn continues.

'That's what happened to Charlie!' I exclaim. 'So he wasn't really robbed?'

'It was most likely a set-up,' DC Fenn tells me. 'We're trying to raise awareness – to send people into schools to give talks about it, warn of the dangers. But it's a losing battle. I know you were trying to help your friend, Libby, but you could easily have been sucked in deeper. You were carrying drugs to a user. You really should have contacted us, or told someone a lot sooner.'

We find Madz and her mum in the waiting room. 'Are you OK?' Madz asks.

'Exhausted,' I tell her. 'They said I should have gone to the police earlier.'

'They said that to me too,' says Madz. 'We could

have been charged with drug dealing, Libs!'

'What a business.' Madz's mum sounds sad and tired. 'Never imagined our girls would get caught up in something like this. Never.'

'Me neither,' Dad says firmly.

'Carrying drugs, mixing with those people,' Madz's mum goes on. 'Anything could have happened.'

'I know,' Dad says, sighing. 'I'm as shocked as you are.'

'We did call the police in the end,' I remind them both. 'But Madz, I'm sorry I got you involved. I was stupid.'

'No, you weren't,' says Madz. 'You were just trying to help Kyle.'

'Where is Kyle?' I ask. 'Is he still being questioned? We need to wait for him, Dad.'

'I'm afraid he might be a while longer,' says DC Fenn. 'We have a lot of questions for him. His mother isn't well enough to come and we're waiting for an appropriate adult and the duty solicitor.'

'He didn't do anything!' I protest. 'Why does he need a solicitor?'

'We want to question him about the murder of Zak Defoe.'

I almost laugh. 'That's crazy! He had nothing to do with that.'

'We have evidence that suggests that he may have been involved.'

I suddenly feel as if I'm going to keel over. 'I . . . I . . .'

'Sit down here a moment, Libby,' says Dad.

'It can't be him. It can't!' I tell her.

'I'm unable to discuss that with you, I'm afraid,' says DC Fenn.

33

'Kyle didn't do it, Dad,' I insist as Dad guides my hand to the open car. I let Samson jump in before climbing in myself.

Dad gets in and starts the engine. 'Seems pretty dodgy to me. I can't believe you were mixing with someone like that.'

'Dad, he was just trying to help Charlie. Why would he kill Zak?'

'Who knows?' says Dad. 'Maybe he was high on drugs.'

Parents could be so stupid. 'Kyle doesn't take drugs,' I say. 'It must have been Marty. The police haven't found him, have they?'

'The police will look at it from every angle,' says Dad. 'I'm sure they'll work it out.'

The car ride home is strained and silent. It's a relief to get into my room and snuggle up with Samson. I can almost pretend none of it is real. But the peace doesn't last long.

'I'm horrified by all of this,' says Dad, coming into my room. 'I just can't believe you got involved. And I can't understand why you didn't come and talk to me.'

I wish he'd just go away and leave me alone. But I say nothing.

'What if you'd been charged with dealing drugs?' Dad demands. 'That's what you were doing, Libby, even if you felt you had no choice. You heard what that police officer said. I'm not sure you understand how serious this is. You betrayed our trust. And when you were meant to be grounded too! Your mum was so keen to give you more independence, but I was right all along – it was too much, too soon. You weren't ready for it.'

'But Dad –'

'I'll have to discuss appropriate consequences for this with your mum,' Dad interrupts. 'I thought you were sensible. You're lucky nothing worse happened. You could have gone to prison. You could be dead!'

I feel wretched. 'I'm sorry,' I say, tears pricking my eyes. 'I didn't mean any of it to happen.'

'That's as maybe. And it's our fault as much as

yours. We'll just have to start again. We'll get Gran back here for after school every day, like before.'

'There's no need –'

'I think there is,' he says firmly.

I lie in bed that night, comforted only by the sound of Samson's breathing in his bed across the room. It's so hot I'm sleeping just under a sheet, with a fan on lightly too. I wonder where Kyle is now. Are they keeping him at the police station? Is he in a cell?

It was Charlie's note that started all this. If I hadn't given it to Kyle, none of this would have happened.

I wake when Mum comes home – it must be after 11 p.m. Minutes later I can hear Mum and Dad arguing in their bedroom, and I know it's about me. I don't want to hear what they're saying, but their room is next to mine and their voices are too loud to ignore.

'It was your idea to give her all this freedom!' Dad's saying. 'See what happened? She wasn't ready for it. She's too naïve. Not worldly enough.'

'She's not worldly because you and your mother

insist on mollycoddling her!' Mum answers. 'How's she going to learn if she stays at home and goes nowhere?'

'You know I'm not suggesting that! Just one thing at a time.'

'And why weren't you keeping more of an eye on her? I was away – you were here. You should have known exactly where she was and who she was with. That shouldn't be too much to ask!'

'She lied to me,' says Dad.

My heart sinks when I hear him say this. He sounds so deeply disappointed. It's true – I've never lied before, not like this.

'She lied because she knew you wouldn't let her do what she wanted!' says Mum.

'Yes – go off with some strange boy – get involved with drug dealers – traffic drugs around the country? Too right I wouldn't have let her!'

'She's no different from any other teenager and she doesn't want to be,' says Mum. 'All teenagers get into scrapes, push the boundaries. It's normal. All right, this is a bit more serious than a scrape, but I'm sure she never set out to do anything wrong.'

'She isn't like other teenagers,' Dad rants. 'She's

visually impaired. It makes a big difference. The world isn't an easy place for her. She's much more likely to get hurt because she's less able to tell what's going on.'

'And she needs to learn,' Mum repeats. 'She needs to be allowed to make mistakes. We will worry, of course, but we can't wrap her in cotton wool.'

'Well, I think we should ground her for a month,' says Dad. 'I hope she'll learn something from that. And at least she won't come to more harm.'

'Let's not ground her again. I think we should give her a chance,' says Mum. 'I don't want to curb her independence now, when she's beginning to get more confident.'

'I'm not so sure,' says Dad. 'You realise how serious this was? What could have happened?'

'Of course I do. And I'll have a good talk to her and make sure she fully understands. I have to go in early tomorrow, but I'll talk to her when I get back. Let's show her that we have confidence in her.'

'OK, if that's what you think,' says Dad. 'I only hope you're right.'

I am very relieved about the grounding, but still sad that I've let them both down.

*

There's no more news the next day. And it's so hard to get any information. I don't know Kyle's address or home number, and although I ask at school, they won't give it to me. I try ringing the police station, but they say there's nothing they can tell me either.

I try texting Kyle a few times in the hope that he might answer, but there's no reply. I feel his absence in art the next day when the table next to mine remains empty. I paint, but my heart isn't in it.

'How's it going, Libby?' asks Miss Afia.

'I think I've messed it up,' I tell her. 'That bit there – it's not the shape I wanted.'

'Just curve it a little,' she suggests. 'With a few strokes here in a lighter tone.' She guides my hand to the place she means.

I try it. To my relief it is definitely an improvement. But I can't stop thinking about Kyle and hoping he is OK.

'I don't know what to do,' I tell Madz at lunchtime. 'I feel so helpless.'

'Oh, Libby,' says Madz. 'I'm sure Kyle didn't do it.'

I feel restless at home. Gran is back on Dad's

instruction, and she won't even let me go for a walk with Samson. Dad insists he'll walk him later when he gets home. Samson keeps coming over and nuzzling me, wondering what's going on.

'How's it going with Dominic?' I ask Gran, trying to make the best of it.

'I haven't enjoyed myself so much for years,' Gran tells me. 'We're having the best time. We might even go on holiday together in September. It's lovely to have someone, Libby, but it has to be the right boy. This drug dealer of yours – I'm surprised at you. I know beggars can't be choosers, but drugs? Really, Libby, I thought you had more sense.'

I gasp in horror. 'How can you say that? That is so insulting!' This comes out louder than I intend, but I am so angry. 'I'm not a beggar. There's more to me than just blindness, thank you very much. And Kyle's not a drug dealer, or a drug user. He was trying to help a friend, that's all. Which is all I was trying to do too!'

'Oh Libby, there's no need to lose your temper –'

'I haven't lost my temper, but what you said was horrible and untrue and I'm angry.'

'It was a shock, that's all,' says Gran, 'to hear

you've got involved in all that.'

'I wasn't involved,' I repeat.

'Well, I hope you've learned your lesson and will be more careful.'

'I've got homework,' I tell her. I don't want to listen to any more of this.

I go upstairs. I do have homework, but I am not in the mood. So I groom Samson, first massaging his coat with my fingers, which he loves, and then brushing him and gently combing him. I finish by wiping him all over with a damp chamois until his coat is beautifully glossy. Samson is happy and I feel much calmer.

Gran leaves and Dad takes Samson for a walk. I go too. I don't feel like talking, and Dad doesn't say much either. When we get back, I know I must do some homework, but it is so, so hard to concentrate. I cannot stop wondering what's happening to Kyle.

34

It isn't long before I find out.

'Libby!' Madz exclaims as we're walking towards the school entrance the next day. She continues in an excited whisper. 'It's Kyle. He's here.'

'Kyle?' I repeat. 'Where?' I search the blurred shapes of bodies for a taller one, but I'm looking straight ahead and I don't realise he's approaching from the side. I jump when he replies.

'Libby, I'll talk to you later, OK?' His voice is flat.

Later isn't good enough for me. I've been so desperate to speak to him. 'But Kyle,' I reply, 'are you OK?'

'Later.' He moves away, the dark shape of him diminishing against the light floor and walls of the corridor. I feel a chill through my legs even though I was too hot only moments ago. Samson brushes against me, warming and comforting, but I'm still anxious.

'OMG, Libby, he looks dire,' says Madz. 'Washed out. It's like someone's drained all the colour out of him. His eyes, his mouth – they're kind of sinking down his face.'

I shudder at the image. Madz never spares me any details. My heart wrenches for him. 'But they let him go,' I say. 'He's back at school. They can't have charged him with anything, can they?'

'Not with murder, anyway,' says Madz. A bit too loud for my liking.

'You coming to lunch?' Madz asks after history.

'Yeah,' I say. 'Can you see Kyle anywhere?'

'No. But we'll look for him in the dining hall. Do you want to sit with him?'

'Why would I want to eat lunch with Kyle when he doesn't even want to talk to me?' I grumble.

'He said "later" not "never",' Madz points out.

We reach the counter. I can smell the fish and chips, but I'm not sure what else there is so Madz reads me the options. I stick with the fish and chips.

'Oh,' she says. 'I can see him. He's over in the corner on a table full of Year 8s. There are no other spaces. He's looking down and eating. I don't think he wants to talk to anyone.'

That obviously includes me. So I'm surprised when he speaks to me in art.

'Libby,' he says, and I hear the swishing sound as he puts his papers down at the table beside mine.

'Hi,' I say, my fingers tingling as his voice speaks my name.

'I'm sorry about earlier,' he continues, quietly. 'It's all been a bit traumatic and I wasn't sure about coming back to school, what people knew.'

'I've not said anything.'

'Of course not,' he says. 'Listen – are you around after school? Could we go somewhere and talk?'

'The park?' I suggest. Then I remember Gran'll be at home, expecting me back. But I can't go home without hearing what he has to say. I don't like lying again, but I'll have to call Gran with an excuse – and hope she believes me. I feel Samson's tail wagging against me. He heard the word *park*.

'Yeah, that'd be good,' says Kyle.

My heart is beating fast now. And it's more than just wanting to know what happened with the police. It's about being with Kyle.

*

I call Gran as I come out of school.

'I'm meeting up with Jenny, my support worker,' I explain. 'She was meant to come earlier but she's running late and I really need some help with my English. There's a book I can't get in large print or Braille.'

'Of course, Libby,' says Gran. 'Thanks for letting me know. Call me when you're on your way home. Or I can come and pick you up if you prefer?'

'No, I'm fine to walk. And I'll call you when I'm on my way. I promise,' I tell her. I hate lying, but I feel more justified doing it when I think about the horrid things she said yesterday.

'Hi!' Kyle sounds more cheerful, to my relief. I'm also relieved that he didn't hear me lying to Gran.

'He's a good dog that one,' says Kyle, as we walk towards the park. 'I don't like to think what would have happened if Marty hadn't got caught in Samson's lead. I watched it happen – it was like slow motion, the way he lost his footing, keeled over and whacked his head. I know he couldn't have, but it almost looked like Samson was walking round that post with the deliberate aim of tripping Marty.'

'It can't have been deliberate, but it was amazing

all the same,' I tell him. We reach the park and walk towards a bench. I let Samson off for a run. 'What happened to you with the police?'

'They kept me there for twenty-four hours and I thought they'd let me go, but then they got an extension for another twelve. It was awful.'

He pauses. I wait, but he says nothing. So I reach over instinctively and touch his arm, feeling for his hand. He takes my hand in his.

'They think I must know all kinds of stuff,' he continues eventually. 'Stuff that I've no idea about. And worst of all, they think I killed Zak. They've let me go now, while they "pursue their enquiries", but I'm not off the hook.'

'But why do they think it was you?' I ask.

'They found the knife. My prints are on it.'

I gasp in horror. 'Oh Kyle!'

'You sound like you think I did it!' Kyle exclaims.

'Of course not,' I tell him.

'They're not the only prints,' he goes on, 'or they would have charged me already. But they're on it. Remember the knife Zak tried to give me? I dropped it instantly. But that knife – it was the murder weapon.'

'I'll talk to the police,' I suggest. 'I can tell them I was there when Zak tried to give it to you.'

'But Libby, you didn't actually see,' he says gently. 'You can't say for sure that I didn't take it, can you?'

I feel suddenly helpless. 'I wish I could do something,' I say. 'I know you're innocent.'

Kyle squeezes my hand and I squeeze back.

'I read about Zak online,' I comment. 'His parents said he was a good kid, doing well at school until he started skipping lessons and hanging out with someone who got him going up and down the country moving drugs.'

'Yeah,' says Kyle. 'Charlie said Zak wanted out, didn't he? Zak thought I'd be in danger looking for Charlie. Turns out he was right. Only it was him that lost his life.'

'Do you think Marty killed Zak?' I ask.

'I thought he was going to kill us in that warehouse.' Kyle sighs. 'I think it had to be him, but I don't know for sure. I don't know anything.'

'The police need to talk to Marty,' I say.

'He's hiding or long gone,' says Kyle. 'He's clever, Marty. He doesn't care who takes the blame. All I can do right now is wait.'

35

Gran's gone when I get home, but Dad's there, waiting in the hall.

'What's up?' I ask, warily.

'Have you seen Joe?' he demands. 'Did he tell you what he was doing today? He's not here. Your gran was ever so worried. At least you let her know about your meeting.'

I feel a flash of guilt. 'But Joe never goes anywhere,' I say.

'Exactly,' says Dad. 'And he's not answering his phone. As if we haven't had enough trouble with you, now Joe's starting . . .'

At that moment, the front door bangs. I move away from it, relieved that Joe is home and also that it is his turn rather than mine for interrogation.

'Joe! Where have you been?' Dad demands.

'Reptile Club,' says Joe.

'Reptile Club?' Dad repeats. 'It's the first I've

heard of any reptile club.'

'Well that's where I was,' says Joe. 'Hi Libby.'

'Your gran was worried sick!' says Dad.

'I thought she wasn't coming any more. And I thought I'd be back before you, Dad. Sorry about that.'

'Well, next time, please let us know,' says Dad. 'And I'd like to hear more about this reptile club.'

'Yeah, right,' says Joe, sighing. 'Later.'

'Do you want a biscuit?' I ask Joe.

'No, ta,' says Joe. 'I'm going to check on Whiff. He was looking a bit peaky this morning.'

Whiff is a garter snake, named for the stench he sometimes lets off. I leave Joe to it.

'I hear you went to a reptile club,' says Mum later, when we're having dinner.

Joe sighs. 'Why's everyone making such a fuss about it?'

'Because you never go anywhere, Joe,' I remind him.

'It's no big deal,' says Joe. 'You've been nagging me to get out and make more friends, Mum. And now I have.'

'I'm very happy that you've found other people who share your interest,' says Mum. 'It sounds great. We don't want to curb your freedom.'

'Just tell us what you're doing and where you're going, OK?' says Dad. 'Where is this club? How did you find out about it? And why didn't you answer your phone when I called?'

'Forgot to charge it,' says Joe. 'It's not far away – a mate of mine told me about it. Can you just chill? I'm in trouble if I stay in and now I'm getting a grilling for going out. I can't win.'

I hear Joe's chair scrape back, and then his feet on the stairs. It's Dad's turn to sigh.

I knock on Joe's door when I go upstairs. I feel sorry for him, even though I'm relieved it's his turn to get all the questioning instead of me.

'What?' he asks.

'You OK?' I ask. 'Reptile Club sounds good. Right up your street.'

'I found out about it online,' says Joe. 'I chat with other reptile people. There's a guy on there – Paul. He told me about Reptile Club.'

'So you don't actually know him?'

'You're starting to sound like Mum and Dad,'

he protests.

'I didn't mean to. I'm just interested,' I tell him.

'We only just met face to face,' Joe says, 'but I've known him for ages online. He's older than me, but it's cool. It's all cool. He's got tree frogs. He says he'll show me them some time. He's really friendly.'

Joe's phone rings. It sounds like a frog croaking, not his usual ring tone.

'Aren't you going to answer it?' I ask.

'It's not important,' he says. 'It's only Paul. I'll speak to him later.'

Lying in bed that night, I'm thinking about Joe. I wonder if he's lonely. He never seems to have any friends. And now, suddenly, he's finding new people to meet up with – an older guy who's being friendly. He didn't want to speak to him in front of me. Joe says it's a reptile club, but what if it's not? What if he's being sucked in, like Charlie and Zak and Jez? The tree frogs may not even exist. What if this is county lines too? Or some other kind of grooming? I wondered how parents don't spot that their kids are getting into that stuff. But maybe it's happening in my family too, right under our noses.

I'm not going to say anything to Mum and Dad. Not yet. There must be some way I can check this out for myself.

My phone rings and it's Madz, so I decide to tell her.

'Surely not,' she says.

'He seems happier, but isn't that what it's like at the start?' I say. 'I think he's even got a new mobile – it's a different ring tone. The police said that can be a sign.'

'Ask him,' she suggests.

'He might not even know himself,' I say. 'He may genuinely think he's made a friend, when it's all a trick to suck him in.'

'What do you want to do then – tell your parents?'

'I don't want to jump to the wrong conclusion. I just want to make sure without accusing him, or worrying Mum and Dad. Maybe this is crazy, but I wondered about following him. You'd have to come with me.'

Madz sighs. 'Is that a good idea? Do you really

want to risk getting into trouble again now? And won't he spot us? I mean, I'm not being funny, but you do rather stand out.'

'He's in a dream world. He won't be looking behind him,' I tell her. 'And if he does, we'll just have to act like it's a big coincidence. I don't think he'd ever imagine I'd be following him.'

'I can't believe I'm saying this,' says Madz, 'but OK – I'll come.'

It's the following evening at dinner when Dad helps me out by asking Joe when his next Reptile Club meeting is.

Joe grunts. I wait. Maybe he has a mouthful of chicken.

'Pardon?' Dad says.

'Why are you asking me?' Joe says gruffly. 'You don't want to come, do you?'

'I'm only showing an interest in what you're doing. How often does this group meet?'

'Give me a break, Dad,' Joe moans.

'We're just making conversation.'

'Then let's talk about something else.'

I'm feeling more suspicious now. If it really is a

Reptile Club, then why is Joe so reluctant to talk about it?

'Have you given it up?' Dad asks. 'Aren't you going any more?'

'I'll be giving up on this dinner in a minute,' Joe retorts, 'and going back to my room.'

'Just tell us what's going on,' Dad suggests. 'Then we'll stop asking.'

Joe gives a deep sigh. 'The next meeting is on Wednesday. They meet once a week. Happy now?'

'That wasn't so hard, was it?' says Dad.

Joe huffs. 'I'm taking my dinner upstairs,' he announces, 'where I can eat in peace, in the company of gentle creatures that just accept me as I am.'

'Oh Joe!' Dad protests. But I hear Joe's chair scrape back and the squeak of the kitchen door.

'Hormones, probably,' Dad tuts.

I'm wondering whether to talk to Dad, to tell him my suspicions. But I don't. I might be wrong anyway. And if Dad interferes, Joe will catch on pretty fast and then he might not go wherever he's going. Instead, I text Madz and she says she'll be free on Wednesday to follow him with me.

*

When Wednesday comes, Madz is round at mine after school and we chat in my room, the door partly open so Madz will spot Joe heading out. At 4 p.m. he's clearly getting ready to leave. Madz and I head down too, along with Samson, making out to Joe and Gran that Madz is going home and we're taking Samson for a walk. We give Joe a thirty-second head start. We don't want him to get too far ahead, but neither do we want him to realise we're following. I hope he's not going too far, or this is going to be impossible.

'You were right about him being in a world of his own,' Madz tells me. 'He's got headphones on and he's looking at his phone too.'

We walk for about twenty minutes. Luckily it isn't so hot today, or I'd be worrying about stopping to give Samson a drink.

'He's gone into a café,' Madz tells me. She stops and Samson and I stop too. 'I don't want to go any further or he might see us through the window.'

'What are we going to do?' I ask.

'There's some dodgy looking characters going in,' she says.

I lean against the wall.

'I've got a sun cap in my bag,' Madz tells me. 'I'll put it on and sneak up, see if I can find out what's going on. You wait here. Just don't move. I won't be long.'

I stand there waiting. In the end, I pull my phone from my bag and scroll through, listening to the start of messages. I'm half aware of two people chatting and laughing as they pass.

Then I vaguely hear something that sounds like, 'Did you see that? Pretending to be blind and looking at her phone! Must be in it for the benefits. What a fraud! We should report her.'

I slip my phone back into my bag and stand there, almost shaking with anger. I want to respond, but I feel too scared on my own. I don't know how many of them there are. Tears prick my eyes, even though I can hear Mum's voice telling me, *Be strong, don't let them get to you. They're just ignorant.*

Most of the time I can believe in myself. I am determined to live a full life, to do what I want to do. But then other times I feel scared and I realise I'm in too deep – like now, when I'm on my own and people say horrible things. Right now, I feel like I'm never going to be OK. I'm never going to be like everyone else. Even with Samson, I can't just do what other people do. I shiver. I wish Madz would come back. I have no idea where I am.

36

'Libs!' I'm so relieved to hear Madz's voice. 'Come on, this way.'

'Forward, Samson,' I tell him, and we hurry a little way along the pavement and round a corner. 'Well?' I ask.

'I wasn't sure at first,' she tells me. 'There was Joe and this older guy who was being really friendly to him – and then a couple of others, and a girl too. Then I heard one of them say, "Have you got the stuff?"'

'Was it drugs?' I gasp. 'What happened?'

'He pulled out a package – a padded envelope – but he didn't even try to hide it. He just put it in the middle of the table. Joe started opening it.' Madz suddenly sounds like she's chuckling. 'And then he started dishing out some reptile magazine. They were definitely talking about snakes – the long slithery kind. It all looks legit, Libs.'

'Phew!' I am so relieved. 'Let's go home.'

On the way I tell her what the girls said.

'Just ignore them,' she advises. 'Those people are stupid. You might be blind, but they will NEVER see past the end of their ignorant noses.'

It's about an hour after I'm home and I'm doing homework in my room when Madz texts. '**Call me.**'

I call her. 'What's up?'

'I didn't know whether to tell you this,' says Madz, 'but you'll find out sooner or later.'

'Find out what?' I demand. 'Is this about Kyle?'

'No. It's about you,' she says. 'Those girls you heard. They took a photo of you looking at your phone, with Samson too. It's gone viral on Instagram. People are saying hideous things, Libby – you're a hoax, you shouldn't have a guide dog if you can see and it's all about benefit fraud.'

I feel myself start to shake. 'Why don't people realise there are all kinds of visual impairment and all kinds of levels of it too? Why do they just think "blind" is one thing – seeing nothing?'

'I never understood before I met you,' Madz admits.

'Shall I reply – shall I explain?'

'See what your mum and dad think.'

But I don't want to wait to talk to them about it. I scroll through Instagram and am shocked. The comments read aloud by the automated voice sound so brutal that I want to cry. I start a very angry reply, but then change it to a simple explanation of my condition and the things I can and cannot see and how Samson helps.

I hear the door open and shut. Mum's back.

'I had a meeting that finished early so I thought I'd come home,' she says. 'Is everything all right?'

Tears slide down my face as I tell her about the photo on Instagram and the comments. Mum is horrified, and really angry too.

'How dare they?' she exclaims. 'Let me have a look.'

While she takes out her phone, I nervously check Instagram again. I am surprised and touched to listen to a stream of supportive replies to my post – some from other visually impaired people and others from people who were upset by the earlier comments. I am so relieved.

'I can't believe some people,' Mum exclaims.

'But I think you've handled it really well. Look at all those people coming out in your support. Good on you, girl!'

I still feel too distracted to do any homework. Instead, I browse back through the flower photos on my computer – zooming in so I can see the colours and shapes. I start to feel calmer. I come to pictures I can't place for a moment. This was after Harwell House. Then I realise – it was the path to the station, the day we found Zak's body. When I was trying to distract myself while we were waiting for the police.

Some of the pictures I like a lot, though I've also sometimes clicked accidentally and have pictures of the grass and the path – but not, thank goodness, the body. There's a speck of white in one picture that makes me zoom in. It's not a petal – it has a square corner. It looks more like a small piece of paper. I zoom in further. I think there's writing but I can't make it out. I don't know if it's blurred anyway, or if it's my eyes.

It's a scrap of paper. But what if it was something significant? Isn't that an 'M' on it? What if it was something of Marty's – evidence that he was there? It's not likely, I know. Even if it was Marty's, it wouldn't be proof that he killed Zak. I want to email the photo to Kyle to have a look, but first I want to know what it says.

'Joe!' I call. 'Come here a mo.'

'What?' he says, and I turn to see his shape in the doorway.

'Are you holding a reptile?' I ask, getting a whiff of something.

'Only Drake.' Drake is a leopard gecko.

'Can't you put him back? I don't want him loose in here and I want you to look at something – tell me what it says.'

'Drake's cool, don't worry. I won't let go of him,' says Joe. 'Show me.'

I point to the screen, where I've blown up the image of the scrap of paper as big as it will go. 'What does that say?'

Joe comes closer. 'Looks like a receipt,' he tells me. 'It's a bit blurry.'

'But can you read it?' I ask eagerly.

'Hold Drake a mo and I'll have a closer look. There's definitely numbers and letters.' The creature is lowered into my hands, its claws digging slightly as if it doesn't trust me not to drop it.

'It looks like Walkers crisps and Coke – one can – and the prices. Oh, and it says Sainsbury's Local at the top. And there's the date: June 16th. Is it important?'

I shrug. 'I thought it might be, but that doesn't sound very significant, even though it's the right date. I thought it was an M, but I was looking upside-down – it's a W. Here – take Drake. I don't think he likes me.'

'Oh!' Joe exclaims, as I feel Drake lifted from my hand.

'Oh what?'

I can hear Joe laughing. 'Just don't move.'

'Why?' I get a whiff of something foul. 'Don't tell me . . . He hasn't?'

'Yeah, he's done a poo. So sorry, Libs. It's just on your top. I'm getting a tissue.'

'Oh Joe. That's gross!'

I don't phone Kyle until I'm in clean clothes and have scrubbed my hands. 'I found something in a photo,' I tell him. 'One I took when I found Zak's body. I thought it might be evidence, but it turns out it's just a Sainsbury's receipt. Not much use.'

'Shame,' says Kyle. 'Maybe you should let the police have it anyway. Just in case.'

'Won't they laugh at me?' I say.

'Why should they?'

I still feel reluctant, but it could be a good excuse to call. I doubt they'll tell me anything, but it's worth a try.

'Can you email it to us?' DC Fenn asks, once I explain. 'We'll certainly have a good look at it. I'm sure we don't have that receipt on our file, so it may well have blown away after you photographed it. You were sensible to tell us. Often people think the evidence they have is no use, but it can turn out to be the missing clue.'

'And will you let me know?'

'If I can,' she says.

'How's the enquiry going?' I ask hopefully. 'I know Kyle's innocent, and he's stressed out by all this. Have you found Marty?'

'I'm sorry, but there's not much I can divulge at the moment,' says the policewoman. 'We are still looking for Marty, but we're pursuing other lines of enquiry too. If there is any information you can give us about the whereabouts of Charlie Smithson, please let us know.'

I flinch. 'You don't think *Charlie* did it?'

'We would like to talk to him, that's all. Like Marty, he seems to have disappeared. We're doing our best to get to the bottom of it all, I promise.'

I work the rest of the afternoon, but keep stopping to think about everything. I've been so wrapped up with worrying about Kyle that I haven't been thinking so much about Charlie. I wonder where he is right now. And I wonder where Marty is too. I wish the police would find him.

When my phone rings, I jolt in the chair and grab it quickly. It's only Madz. I tell her about the receipt.

'Shame it wasn't something that would prove Marty was there,' she agrees.

'I'm scared they think Charlie did it,' I say. 'Madz, you don't . . . you don't think it could have been Charlie, do you?'

'I can't say it hasn't crossed my mind, Libs,' Madz admits.

37

The following morning I'm getting dressed for school with the radio on. That's when I hear that a boy has been charged with the murder of Zak Defoe.

'The boy is under eighteen so cannot be named,' the reporter announces.

Panic rises in my throat. I fling my arms around Samson and cling to him so tight he squeezes out of my grip and moves away. Under eighteen means it can't be Marty.

I call Kyle. I'm holding my breath as the phone rings on without an answer. It can't be Kyle. It can't. But there's no reply.

I call Madz. 'Did you hear?' I demand. 'They've charged someone — someone under eighteen. I'm worried about Kyle. He's not answering his phone.'

'Oh Libs — can you call the police? Will they tell you?'

'I can try. I don't know . . .'

There's a beep on my line – someone is trying to get through. 'I have to go,' I tell Madz.

'Libby?'

I am so relieved to hear Kyle's voice that I throw my head back and it hits the wall, which was closer than I thought. 'Ow!'

'You OK?'

'Bumped my head,' I tell him, rubbing the spot. 'But my head's used to it. Did you hear they've charged someone?'

'Yeah, but I don't know who. I'm off the hook, and to be honest that's all I care about. They believe me now. They know I wasn't involved.'

'Do you think it's Charlie?' I ask.

'I don't want to think so,' says Kyle. 'But he did run off fast, didn't he?'

'Why would he kill Zak?' I ask. 'Do you think Marty might've paid him to do it?'

'I'm sure he wouldn't have done it unless he was forced to,' says Kyle. 'Maybe it was another empty promise. Perhaps Charlie thought it was the only way out.'

'But *murder*?' I don't want to believe it.

'Maybe Charlie and Zak just had beef and it all

went wrong,' says Kyle. 'Zak might've had the knife on him. Maybe he pulled it on Charlie, and Charlie tried to get it off him and ended up stabbing him. But even if Charlie did it, it's Marty who got them into that mess, and it's Marty who should go down for it.'

'Can you be forced to stab someone?' I ask.

'People can end up doing things they'd never imagine when they feel under threat. That's why no one should carry knives, isn't it?'

'If only we'd found Charlie sooner,' I groan. 'If he did it, he might be in prison for the rest of his life. He must have felt he had no option.'

'It's still no excuse,' says Kyle.

'Can we find out who the police have charged?' I ask. 'I'm going to call and ask.'

'Let me know what they say,' Kyle says.

DC Fenn knows exactly why I'm calling and she's not giving much away. 'I can tell you this,' she says. 'That receipt in your photo turned out to be rather significant after all.'

I'm surprised. 'Really? How?'

'After you gave us the photo of that receipt, we checked the CCTV footage at the Sainsbury's Local.

A boy was buying Coke and crisps only ten minutes before Zak Defoe was stabbed. The time matches that on the receipt.'

'Who?' I ask nervously. I hold my breath. 'Charlie?'

'No,' she says. 'The person we've charged was already a suspect. We'd questioned him, and he'd denied being in the area at all. Your dropped receipt appeared to prove that he was there. And we now have further evidence. A partial print on the knife.'

I'm so full of relief that it wasn't Charlie, I barely hear what she's saying. But if it's not Kyle or Charlie, who is it? Marty's too old. If it's someone from that house, it can't be Reuben. So that only leaves . . .

'Jez?' I ask. 'It's Jez, isn't it?'

I hear her sigh. 'I can neither confirm nor deny that is the name of the person involved.'

'Jez,' I repeat.

But she won't tell me anything more.

'I bet Marty sent Jez to get Zak back, and Zak wouldn't come,' says Kyle when I call to share the news. 'Marty's got a lot to answer for. They think he's left the country.'

'He should be in prison,' I say furiously. 'It's not right.'

'I hope they put him away one day,' says Kyle.

'So do I,' I tell him. 'I'm just glad they know you're innocent, and Charlie too.'

'Me too,' says Kyle.

I wait for him to say something else, but he doesn't.

39

It's Friday the next day. I'm at school coming out of French when I hear Kyle's voice.

'Libby, I wondered if you'd like to go for a meal,' he says. 'To celebrate?'

Even though I was hoping we'd stay friends, this takes me by surprise. Is he actually asking me out?

'I'd like to,' I say, aware that my long pause might be interpreted the wrong way. 'I just don't know if I'll be allowed. My parents aren't convinced that you didn't drag me into everything. Maybe if they meet you? But they still might not agree . . .'

'I'm happy to meet them,' says Kyle. 'But I'll understand if they say no.'

After school, I'm in the kitchen, pouring myself a glass of juice and thinking about Kyle, when Joe comes in.

'She's not well,' he tells me.

I'm suddenly wondering if there was another

reason why Mum came home early the other day. 'Is she ill? Did she tell you?' I ask.

'She's acting weird. I think something's wrong,' says Joe. 'But she can't exactly tell me, can she?'

'Why not?'

'Libby! I'm being serious here!'

'So am I!'

'That's nice of you,' he says, his voice softening. 'Will you hold her for a sec while I phone the vet?' Scaly skin brushes my hand. I lurch backwards. 'Careful,' he says. 'Here, Tallulah. You're OK. Libby will hold you.'

'What the heck, Joe!' I find myself with a bearded dragon in my hands. 'I thought you were talking about Mum!'

'Mum's not ill, is she?'

'I just . . . never mind,' I say.

Next thing I hear, he's on the phone to the vet.

'They said to bring her in,' he tells me. 'I'm just gonna text Dad to see when he'll be home. I hope he can take me.'

'But Joe . . .'

Great. He's left me holding Tallulah. She's so still in my hands, I think she may be trying to play dead.

Some reptiles do that when they feel threatened. I've learned that from Joe, though I'm not sure about bearded dragons. Then I panic. She isn't dead, is she? I cradle her gently against my chest so I can use my right hand to run across her rough skin until I can feel her heart beating. At least, I think it's her heart and not my pulse. She shifts a little. Phew. She's definitely still alive.

Joe's back quickly, to my relief. 'Dad's going to come straight home. I told him it was urgent,' he says. 'Here – I'll take her now.'

I am relieved to hand her back. Joe doesn't speak, but I can hear the stress in his fast breaths. Tallulah was his first reptile and, even though I can't imagine feeling attached to a scaly creature like this, I know she's important to Joe.

'I'm sure she'll be OK,' I tell him. 'I know she's special to you.'

'Your ambulance awaits,' says Dad, rushing through the front door. 'Where's the patient? No stretcher needed, I hope?'

'She's here,' says Joe. 'We're ready. I'll just put her in the carrier.'

No sooner have Joe and Dad gone than I hear a

key in the door.

'Did you forget something?' I ask.

'What?' It's Mum's voice. 'I've got to prepare my talk for next week and I thought I might as well do it in the comfort of my own home. Come here and hug me!'

We have a lovely hug. I explain about Tallulah.

'Gosh, I know how much Joe loves that creature,' says Mum. 'I hope she'll be OK.'

I don't often get Mum to myself, so I take a deep breath and make the most of it. 'Mum, I know you were right in what you said to me – when I went out with Kyle and didn't tell you. I've learned my lesson. I'd never do anything like that again.'

'I'm glad to hear it,' says Mum.

'So,' I go on, still half holding my breath. 'Is there any chance you'd let me go out with him? He's asked me to go out for a meal.'

Mum sounds aghast. 'You want to go out with him after everything –'

'The only thing he's guilty of is trying to help a friend,' I interrupt. 'He's *nice*, Mum. He had nothing to do with drug dealing – nothing at all. Please meet him and judge for yourself.'

There's a pause. 'In that case, I'm happy to meet him,' she says.

I give her another hug.

'You know,' she adds, 'I think it's time me and your dad went out for a meal too. We haven't been out, just the two of us, for ages.'

Dad is soon back with Joe and Tallulah, and some medicine that should sort her out. I hear Mum and Dad later, discussing a night to go out together – and I'm glad.

It feels really awkward when Kyle comes to meet my parents. It's as if he's asking their permission to marry me or something, when we're only going for a bite to eat.

Dad gets his teacher hat on and starts asking about how he's doing at school, and I cringe inside. Mum asks him about his family, and he tells her about his mum. Then the conversation kind of runs out.

'Has he passed the test?' I ask them after he's gone.

'He does seem like a nice boy,' says Mum.

I text Kyle and he replies with a happy face emoji – just the one.

273

I get a message from Madz, asking if I want to go to the cinema. I reply saying that I'm going out with Kyle.

She phones me instantly. 'You're going *out* with him?' she asks. 'And I'm sure you said you weren't interested in dating! Isn't that what you said when I started seeing Ollie?'

'True,' I say. 'I didn't plan this. But I do really like Kyle.'

'He's a lot nicer than Ollie,' says Madz. 'I'll try not to be too jealous. You'll have to tell me all about it on Monday.'

I feel a buzz of excitement. 'I will. I promise,' I tell her.

40

'What kind of food do you like?' Kyle asks me, as we sit in the park with Samson running around nearby, his bell jingling gently. 'Where shall we go to eat?'

'I don't mind. I like most things,' I tell him.

'That's not very helpful.'

Samson gives a gentle snort — or it could be a snore.

'I know Samson likes the smells at McDonalds,' says Kyle, 'but I think we can do better than that. I want to treat you.'

'You don't have to pay for me,' I tell him.

'No, but I want to. Do you like Chinese? I know a good place.'

'Yes, I do,' I tell him. 'I'm not too good with chopsticks though. And duck pancakes are a bit fiddly.'

'Then how about Oakingtons?' he says. 'They've got all sorts. I've never been, but I've heard it's nice food.'

'That'd be great,' I tell him, 'though you may have to read me the menu.'

'No problem,' he says. 'I'll see you tonight.'

I'm feeling excited when I set out with Samson to meet Kyle, and I'm enjoying wearing the new top I bought with Madz.

'Hiya,' calls Kyle, as we reach the corner. 'Like your top.'

'Thanks.' I feel awkward. I'm not used to compliments from boys. If there are any compliments going, they're usually aimed at Samson.

We reach the restaurant and Kyle holds the door open. I step inside with Samson and wait, hearing the door ping behind me as Kyle comes in too.

'I've booked,' Kyle tells someone I can't see. 'Table for two.'

'You'll have to leave the dog outside,' I hear someone say. 'No dogs in here, sorry.'

'He's a guide dog,' I say. 'You have to allow guide dogs. He won't be any bother. He'll just sit under the table.'

'I'm sorry – I have to think of other customers,' the man says firmly.

276

'This is mad!' says Kyle.

'It's against the law,' I tell the man.

'Then get a solicitor,' he says, sounding as if he couldn't care less.

'Wait a minute,' says Kyle. 'This isn't right. You can't . . .'

'Come on,' I tell him. 'I don't want to eat here anyway – not with someone like that.'

'Pathetic!' says Kyle. 'You're right. Let's go.'

'I can't believe it,' says Kyle, when we're back outside. 'I'm so sorry, Libby. I should have checked first.'

'You shouldn't need to,' I say wearily. 'He's breaking the law. Don't worry, I'll report him.'

'Where shall we go then?' he asks. 'I was really looking forward to that.'

I feel a tug from Samson.

Kyle laughs. 'He's pointing his nose at McDonalds two doors down.' he says.

'That's fine with me,' I say.

'It wasn't what I had in mind,' says Kyle. 'But OK.'

Samson speeds so eagerly towards the doors, I have to walk fast to keep up. The noisy chatter inside suggests it's busy.

'You sit down and I'll order,' Kyle says. He guides me and I keep my free arm close to my body to avoid whacking anyone as I pass. I hear comments from children about Samson.

'Look at that dog! Can I have a dog, Mum? I want one just like that.'

I hear someone whisper back, 'She's blind. The dog shows her the way.'

'Can it talk?' the child queries. 'Is the dog going to order her food for her? I bet that dog *can* talk. I bet he can say burger or nuggets. You can, can't you, doggie?'

Kyle laughs. 'Reminds me of Reuben.'

'I hope he's got some help,' I say. 'It was awful how they used him and just pretended to be his friends.'

'I hope so too,' says Kyle. 'I saw Tia yesterday. Asked her if they've heard from Charlie, but they haven't. I hope he's OK.'

'It's weird,' I comment. 'We spent all that time looking for him and he's still missing. We don't know if he found his dad. He could even still be working for Marty.'

Kyle snorts. 'Not after everything we went through. What d'you want to eat?'

The good thing here is I know the menu. I don't have to ask Kyle what the options are or get him to tell me what's where on my plate. It's a relief really. I order a veggie burger, fries and a diet Coke.

While we eat, Kyle talks about a trip the art department are doing to Spain.

'I'm thinking about going,' he says. 'My mum said I can. It's not cheap, but the school can offer a subsidy as Mum's on benefits. How about you?'

'Spain?' I exclaim. 'I don't think I'm ready for something like that. After everything that's happened – I don't always feel so safe, even here. In another country, where I don't even speak the language, how would I manage? Everything would be different. And look how I got treated in that restaurant. I've no idea what the attitudes are to guide dogs in other countries, or the laws.'

'They drive on the other side of the road for a start,' says Kyle. 'But I'd be there, and Samson. You'd have to get him a special pet passport, I think. And I'm sure the school would help to sort out support. It would be amazing if we could both go.'

'I'm not sure I've got the confidence,' I tell him. 'Something bad could happen.'

'Bad things can happen anywhere,' says Kyle, pointedly.

'Will you think about it?' he asks again later, as we come out of McDonalds. I feel his hand touch mine and my fingers tingle. 'I'd love it if you came.'

'I'll think about it,' I promise. And I know in my heart that I do want to go. Samson comes between us and lays his nose on our hands. I think he wants to come too.

41

It's August – two months since Jez was charged with murder, but it could be another three or four months until the court case. Marty has gone AWOL. We haven't heard anything about Charlie. I often think about him and wonder, hoping that he's OK.

I'm still seeing Kyle and I'm going on the Spain trip in October too. Mum and Dad have paid the deposit. I'm going to have meetings with Jenny, my support worker, and with Gina, my guide dog mobility instructor too, to prepare for it. Madz has her eyes on a new boy, Jamie, and never stops talking about him. She's told me that if she does go out with him, she's not going to let him walk all over her, like Ollie did.

I'm out with Samson, down the path near the station, looking for flowers to photograph. I've just zoomed in on a pink flower, but it's withered, past its best. I'm suddenly aware that my name's being called.

I turn back the way I've come.

'Libby! Libby! I've got something for you.'

It's a girl's voice, but I don't recognise it. 'Who are you?' I ask, feeling embarrassed.

'Sorry – it's Tia, Charlie's sister.'

'Oh! Tia! Have you heard from Charlie?' I ask, eagerly.

'I haven't seen him,' she said. 'He called though, and spoke to Mum. He's found his real dad – and he's staying with him in Birmingham.'

I feel almost like I could clap for joy and a warmth goes right through me.

'I hoped so much that would happen,' I tell her. 'Did he say how it's going?'

'His dad's divorced, living on his own, and he and Charlie have hit it off, so he says,' Tia answers. 'Mum hopes a change of scene will keep him out of gangs and away from drug dealing. He's going to start at a new school there. And my dad's back home with us.'

'I hope Charlie will be OK and sort himself out,' I say.

'Me too,' she says. 'Anyway, he sent this and asked me to give it to you.'

She's holding something out and I take it. It's an envelope.

'He doesn't want me to give it to someone, does he?' I ask warily.

'Nothing like that!' she exclaims. 'I think he just wanted to thank you, and to say sorry for getting you and Kyle involved. He never meant to drag you into all that. Look, I've gotta go. Will you be able to read it, or do you want me to read it to you?'

I tell her that I will be able to read it with a magnifier when I get home. Then she's gone. I stroke Samson's warm back. He nuzzles against me and we stand there for a few moments. I hold the envelope, running my finger along the flat straight edge, then I put it in my pocket. Samson and I walk on together down the path. Something bright is waving in the breeze on the grass verge.

'Stand, Samson,' I say. He stops. I move closer, crouching down. It's a wild flower – something yellow, with glossy petals that shimmer in the sunlight. I take out my camera, lean in – and click.

ACKNOWLEDGEMENTS

So many people have helped me in writing this book and I want to thank all of you profusely. First, of course, my fabulous editors, Sarah Levison, Liz Bankes and Stella Paskins – as well as all the lovely people at Egmont who have been involved with this book at every level. I would also like to thank my wonderful agent, Anne Clark, for all her support.

This book was inspired by Emily Davison and her guide dog, Unity, when we met at A Place at the Table – a conference organised by Inclusive Minds, a collective for people who are passionate about inclusion, diversity, equality and accessibility in children's literature. Emily is an Inclusive Minds Ambassador and among other things she talked about her hobby, photography. I immediately thought a visually impaired teenager who loves photography would make a great character for a YA novel. I discussed the idea with Emily and she said, 'Your novel and character sound really fantastic!'

In my work with people with disabilities I have worked with people with visual impairments, but it was crucial to me to do as much research as possible and to get feedback at every stage of writing.

Inclusive Minds put me in touch with Cathy Wright who teaches at Worcester College for the Blind. I was welcomed there for an overnight stay, where I met and discussed ideas with students. I also got to explore the wonderful Braille Library and to talk in assembly about my work as an author. Students from the college read and gave valuable feedback once the manuscript was complete. I thank you all, but in particular Amy and Mustafa. I'd also like to thank Reeah Seevoosurrun, a student at Chancellor's School, who helped me with early research as well as giving feedback later.

Special thanks also go to Tim Howell of The Guide Dog Training School, Redbridge for giving me the opportunity to visit the school and also for reading the manuscript and giving valuable feedback, and to Sam, guide-dog trainer, for taking me out with two lovely dogs to experience the training for myself.

I would also like to thank Iryna Pona of The Children's Society and Loran Kingston, Community Safety Intervention Officer for help with other aspects of the story line, as well as Kevin N. Robinson for advice on police procedures, and Paul, from Paul's Reptile Den, for help with reptile research.

Any errors are my own and not the fault of anyone acknowledged here.

Thanks to everyone else who gave me feedback and especially fellow members of our long-running Friday workshop: Angela Kanter, Jo Barnes, Vivien Boyle and Derek Rhodes.

Last but by no means least, I thank my husband Adam and my children Michael and Zoe for all the support they have given me – especially at times when I have been intensely focused on writing and editing and oblivious to much else!

USEFUL CONTACTS

Missing People
www.missingpeople.org.uk

The Children's Society
www.childrenssociety.org.uk

ChildLine
www.childline.org.uk
0800 1111

Guide Dogs (The Guide Dogs for The Blind Association)
www.guidedogs.org.uk

Emily Davison: youtube.com/user/ fashioneyesta
www.fashioneyesta.com

To report a crime and other concerns that do not require an emergency response call 101. Always call 999 in an emergency.

Crimestoppers – a free confidential service where you can report information about a crime anonymously. Freephone: 0800 555 111

How do you catch a killer when you can't move and have no voice?

I HAVE NO SECRETS

PENNY JOELSON

WINNER
OF MULTIPLE AWARDS, INCLUDING
THE CHILDREN'S BOOK AWARD
(OLDER READERS)

I know what I saw.

I didn't imagine her.

· WHO IS SHE?

GIRL IN THE WINDOW

PENNY JOELSON

HIGH VOLTAGE READING

EUGENE LAMBERT

THE LONG FOREVER

Good Girl, Bad Blood

HOLLY JACKSON

The No.1 New York Times bestselling author of
A Good Girl's Guide to Murder

SOMEDAY
DAVID LEVITHAN

The sequel to the New York Times bestselling EVERY DAY

A VERY Large Expanse of Sea

New York Times bestselling author
TAHEREH MAFI

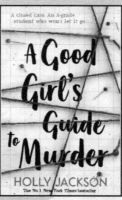

A closed case. An A-grade
student who won't let it go...

A Good Girl's Guide to Murder

HOLLY JACKSON

The No.1 New York Times bestseller

MY NAME IS RUBY

I AM NOT A NUMBER

LISA HEATHFIELD

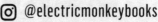

YA READING FROM ELECTRIC MONKEY

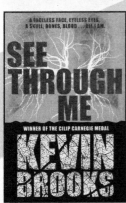